FADE ROUTE

Books by David Chill

Post Pattern

Fade Route

Bubble Screen

Safety Valve

FADE ROUTE

A Novel By

DAVID CHILL

For Matthew

One

The last time I saw Wayne Fairborn alive he was with a sultry blonde in a tight orange miniskirt. Her name was Nina Lovejoy and she was young and vivacious. She was also the last person Wayne should have accompanied. Nina slipped an arm playfully inside the crook of his and they strolled upstairs towards his office. Even if Wayne had been a freewheeling bachelor, the spectacle would have raised eyebrows. In fact, he was both a married man and an aspiring political candidate and he should have had the good sense to be discreet.

Wayne and I had been sitting together in the workshop room of Second Chance. The room was sparsely decorated, appropriate for a setting designed to assist those down on their luck. I glanced out the window and saw the last golden traces of the sunset. It was disappearing into the Pacific, about to be replaced by the gloom of a moonless black night. It was almost seven o'clock and the only thing in Southern California that let you know summer was ending were the shorter days. The temperature was an awful seasonal gauge. The autumn winds which blew sporadically through the region were generally hot and dry.

Wayne took a sip from a bottle of soda and leaned towards me. "I may need to use your services, Burnside," he said.

I nodded. "Someone trying to assassinate you already?"

He pondered that question a bit too long. "Not exactly."

I turned and looked closely at his face. The handsome features revealed no turbulence within. If he were not a politician, he'd probably excel as a professional poker player. He was tall and fit and his square jaw exuded confidence. His blue eyes were as light and clear as an August sky.

"Can you expand on that?" I asked.

Wayne looked off in the distance. "Burnside," he began, "sometimes I wish I had a job like yours."

I looked at him incredulously and sighed. Everyone had such a colored view of the vaunted life of the private eye. A life of action, danger, and excitement, punctuated by hot blondes and dead bodies. Immortalized by Humphrey Bogart and Jack Nicholson. I tried to tell people if real life were like the movies, I'd have been killed a dozen times over by now.

"Here's an idea," I suggested. "I'll swap lives with you. I could handle falling asleep to the sound of the waves crashing on the sand. And hobnobbing with people who want to donate money to me in exchange for a favor to be named later. If you want to throw Crystal into the package as well, I wouldn't turn my nose up."

"I might easily make the same offer for Gail," he said, referring to my girlfriend of the past year. I winced as I thought of her.

"You'll have a long commute," I said. "She's up in Berkeley. Getting an advanced degree on how to become a professional thug."

"I thought she was in law school."

"She is."

Wayne laughed a little wistfully and peeled some of the label from his bottle. "I imagine the grass is always greener."

"It shouldn't be for you," I countered.

Indeed not. Wayne Fairborn was a man who was independently wealthy. He was the grandson of a real estate investor who developed a large parcel of land in the suburbs of Los Angeles. A century ago this was considered to be rural countryside; today the area is known as the San Fernando Valley. After his father died a few years ago, Wayne closed down the development office, sold off most of the remaining properties and opened Second Chance in Bay City. He was the embodiment of the good Samaritan who wanted to help people to help themselves.

"To put things in proper perspective," I said, "let me tell you what I did today. My client is a fifty-five year old dermatologist who's convinced that Violet, his twenty-five year old wife, is playing around."

"Is she?"

"Not that I've learned. My morning was spent following this young thing around Malibu, watching her shop for linen and get her nails done. In the afternoon she worked out with a private trainer and then went off to the beach."

He looked at me sadly. "You're ruining my image of you."

I leaned back in my chair. I had met Wayne when I volunteered at Second Chance last year. He impressed me with his dedication and commitment, and with the fact that he had jettisoned a cushy lifestyle to try and make a difference in the world. I had felt a little uneasy with him at first, until it dawned on me that his generosity was sincere. He didn't seem like the type of guy I would pal around with, but then again I don't pal around with many people. Wayne, like me, was something of an enigma. Neither of us fit a mold.

As it turned out though, Wayne had also graduated from USC and remembered me from my days on the gridiron as a safety for the Trojans. Even though it's been almost twenty years, I still get recognized now and then. When Wayne and I first met, we talked about our favorite games, and the ice began to melt away. His brother-in-law, Rusty Haas, who was giving the final speech tonight at the Second Chance orientation, had played for Notre Dame, a team which my crew had beaten in a down-to-the-wire nail biter. The USC-Notre Dame series was considered the greatest cross-sectional rivalry in college football. As such, Rusty's school was hardly one of my favorites, nor was it Wayne's. The two of us began discovering some common ground.

Rusty finished his presentation and everyone was invited to stay for sandwiches and coffee. Metal chairs scraped the cement floor and people began shuffling around. I looked at Wayne and suggested that we adjourn to the hallway to discuss his situation further. He nodded and followed me. I asked him what was really bothering him.

"It's rather difficult to put into words," he said.

"Getting pushed around by the local bully, are you?"

He smiled weakly, and ran his fingers through his sandy blond hair. "In a way, perhaps. You probably haven't had to deal with bullies in your life, Burnside. A tough guy like you."

"I wasn't always this tough," I said, thinking back to the time when an older kid, Otis Miller, did indeed push me around the junior high playground. By the time I was in high school, I was lifting weights and had made the football team. I decided it was time to make up for past slights. I knocked on Otis' door but all I found was his kid brother who told me Otis had been shipped off to military school. I briefly considered thrashing the younger Miller just for the record, but quickly decided the act wouldn't be very gallant.

"Is it related to the campaign?" I asked.

Wayne shrugged. "Maybe."

"You know, people typically hire me because of problems with their marriage, their business or their vices."

"Maybe in this case it's all three," he said, his eyes looking down at the floor.

We sat in silence for a few minutes. A few volunteers walked by and said good night. There were about five of us old-timers at the orientation, and we were there to prep the twenty or so newcomers on how to assist the homeless in the Second Chance way. They were all dressed professionally and in good spirits, their eagerness brimming. In addition, Eddy and Raff were there as well. The two of them were Second Chance clients who had attended a resume workshop a few weeks earlier and had secured temporary janitorial jobs at the Center. I made a mental note to ask how their job search was going.

"If you want my help," I said, turning back to Wayne, "you've got to talk to me. And trust me."

Wayne took a deep breath like a man who was about to dive underwater for a prolonged period. "The campaign is fine. We fielded another poll a few days ago, and the results indicated the race is still a dead heat. We think Mayor Callison's running scared."

"He's been in office a long time. That's quite a testimony to your efforts."

"Callison has a lot of negatives he's working against. Plus, I'm a new face. Outsider and all that."

"That's L.A. for you, and especially Bay City. We love things that are new. We also get bored easily, so don't plan on being loved forever. It's fleeting as hell."

Wayne smiled. "You know, Burnside, you don't bullshit around. Most of the people I know couldn't be candid if their lives depended upon it. You speak your mind. I liked that about you from the start."

"You're in the minority. Most people think my comments grate on them too much."

"For me, it's refreshing. That's why I appreciate your company. See what I mean? Your job is to be envied. I'd love to be able to just say whatever I feel without any compunction."

"Point made," I said and shifted my back against a wall. The silence was making Wayne squirm. He took another deep breath and let it out in a loud whoosh.

"I guess I'll have to trust you," he finally managed. "But this can't go anywhere else."

"Trustworthiness. It's one of my nobler qualities."

He nodded. "The problem," he said with a sigh, "is related to Crystal."

I frowned. "Go on."

"Somebody tried to run her off the road the other night."

The frown turned into a gape. Crystal was a sweet person and not the type who was likely to incur anyone's wrath.

"She was on her way home from a fundraiser," Wayne said, rubbing the bridge of his nose, "and somebody must have followed her down through Coldwater Canyon. It happened when she was driving along a narrow stretch of Sunset. It was late, and some SUV pulled alongside and tried to run her off the road. Scared the hell out of her."

It was now my turn to take a deep breath. Someone had tried to do the same thing to me last year and it was attempted murder. I was lucky to get out of it alive. But I had been investigating a serious case and was being targeted. Crystal's situation might have been very different, so I tried to ease Wayne's mind.

"Maybe it was just road rage."

Wayne shook his head. "I don't know. The guy was tailgating her for miles and he could have passed her any number of times. I'll tell you, she was pretty hysterical. I almost called the doctor to get something to calm her down."

"Any thoughts as to who might have been involved?"

Wayne shook his head again. "I don't know. It might have been Callison's people but there's really no hard evidence here. And with the election a month away, I don't want this to get out."

"You're afraid the press might question why someone was after the candidate's wife?"

"That. Or did the wife simply have a few drinks, crash her car and make up the whole story to cover herself? True or not, the incident could be a huge problem if it became public."

Wayne paused as a few people walked past us towards the exit. The crowd was beginning to thin and somebody called out Wayne's name. It was in a voice as sugary and tantalizing as the package it came in. We turned as a vision of loveliness approached wearing an orange dress with a white linen blazer.

The bottom of her jacket was about two inches above the hemline of her dress.

"You're looking well today, Nina," Wayne remarked slowly, scanning her body like it was a vintage Corvette.

Nina offered up a pixie smile. "I always try to look my best," she said in a delightful voice.

"You know, we're only supposed to motivate these people to get off the streets."

"Let me tell you what I think," she giggled.

"This I have to hear."

Nina tossed her long blonde hair back, the golden strands shimmering in the bright hall lighting. "If I look really hot," she said, "the men and women who come through here will try that much more to help themselves. I mean, I won't go out with any of these guys but at least it'll get them thinking. If they get a job and make some money, then they can get a girl of their very own. And the women can be inspired by me as well. Good plan?"

"Intriguing psychological premise," he mused.

"Wayne, there's something else I wanted to speak with you about," she said, and then looked at me. "Burnside, do you mind?"

I showed her a pair of open palms. "Be my guest."

"Why don't we go upstairs to my office," he suggested and then turned to me. "Say pal, would you mind waiting around for a few more minutes? You and I should really finish our conversation."

"No problem," I said. Time was a commodity I had a lot of these days. As they walked up the stairs, I noticed a bulge around Wayne's ankle and what looked like a holster. Having spent thirteen years with the LAPD, the sight wasn't startling. On Wayne Fairborn however, a gun was definitely out of place.

I went over and helped myself to a sandwich and a cup of coffee. This was my first solid food since breakfast, my case having kept me busy for most of the day. The dermatologist's wife didn't bother to stop for lunch today so neither did I. The sandwich was wolfed down in about three bites and I decided to take another.

"Now there's a man with an appetite," boomed a voice from behind. I turned and saw Eddy Steele strolling towards me. Eddy was an imposing two hundred plus pounds with a dark complexion and mischievous brown eyes.

"Well looky here," I said, shaking his outstretched hand. "How are you?"

"Never better. On the top of my game." He smiled a rich, toothy smile. "Been clean for four weeks now. I'm there, baby, I'm there!"

"Great, Eddy. How's the job hunt coming?"

"Good, real good. I got a couple of definite possibilities," he said, licking his lips. "You helped me a lot."

"Pick up some tips on resume building?"

"I learned me two things at this place," he declared. "I learned what a resume is, and I learned..." He moved closer and lowered his voice. "I learned you have some hot babes walking around here. Mmm-mmm."

I chuckled a little. "Any one in particular catch your eye?"

"That blonde in the orange miniskirt looked mighty good," he said, his eyes sparkling. "I'd do her any time."

"I'm sure she'd be pleased to know that."

"But I think Raff got his eye on her."

My eyebrows shot up. Raff wasn't exactly a carefree playboy. "Where is old Raff? I saw him in here earlier tonight."

Eddy shrugged. "He might still be upstairs finishing up. But he said he had to leave early. I learn not to ask too many questions. Raff kind of a secretive guy."

"You know anything about him?"

Eddy shrugged. "I think Raff let on he was a student last year. Lost his funding or something like that, and had some problems paying rent. He a bright guy when he gets going. He speak real intelligent-like. Know what I mean?"

"Sure, Eddy. When you stop and think about it, nobody's that far from the streets." I gulped and thought about my own dwindling savings account. "It doesn't matter how smart you are or how many degrees you've got. Most people don't have enough savings to last them forever. Once the money runs out, you hit up family, friends, whatever."

"Whatever is right," he agreed. "And when that whatever runs out, you hit the streets."

With that, Eddy stuffed a couple of sandwiches into his jacket pocket and said he'd see me later. Eddy had his share of problems and I wondered if he'd make it. Pulling things together was mostly up to the individual. The ones who controlled their vices seemed better able to escape the streets. The ones who couldn't usually had their fate sealed.

I finished the rest of my sandwich and wandered around the room. Half of the attendees had already left, and it appeared the evening was winding down. In a few seconds I would discover just how wrong that observation would be.

It came without warning as these things are prone to do. There were no shouts, no screams, no tables overturned.

Instead there was just a short pop, not unlike a truck backfiring. The noise was muffled by the sound of plates and glasses clinking and I tried to focus my hearing. A few seconds later I heard another pop, clearer and more distinct. Some people around the room looked up, but most went on eating and talking. I was out the door in an instant however, and raced up the steps. Based on my conversation a few minutes earlier, I had a sick feeling about what I was going to find.

I ran up to the second floor of the building and looked around wildly. To the left of the stairwell was a door that was slightly ajar. To the right were half a dozen cubicles separated by partitions, and an open door which led into a back stairwell facing an alley. I pulled my .38 from its holster and walked carefully along the perimeter of the room.

As I reached the corner office, the smell of cordite wafted into my nostrils. I peeked inside and saw a figure sitting behind a desk. Wheeling around, I leaped into a crouched position and pointed my weapon at them, my left hand steadying the hand with the gun. There was no need; the solitary figure was unable to see me.

In the chair was Wayne Fairborn. His shirt pocket oozed with blood and in his lap sat a business card featuring the logo of a magazine called "Tomorrow's Woman." The title on it read "Assistant Editor." The name on it read "Nina Lovejoy."

Two

It took the paramedics five minutes to arrive, which put them a few minutes ahead of the police. The investigating officer was a plainclothes detective named Barney Sack, a bloated man with curly black hair and a face that could have been composed from silly putty. Depending on how the light hit him, he could appear striking and intense, or opaque and non-descript. I got the feeling if someone stuck a pin in him, he might start to deflate.

Since I was the one who discovered Wayne's body, I was one of the first to be interviewed. Sack had a rumpled look about him, with the top button of his yellow polyester shirt open and the brown rep tie pulled down. At first glance one might think he was working hard, but my guess was he probably left the house each day with this look. He worked for the Bay City Police Department, but he could have been with just about any law enforcement agency. I knew the type. Enough years in a police uniform breeds nothing if not a healthy dose of cynicism.

"Name?" Sack asked, looking down at a clipboard as he chewed the crust of a sandwich.

"Burnside," I answered.

"What time did you find the victim?" he queried, his face still buried in his paperwork.

"About an hour ago."

"Did you know Fairborn well?"

"Somewhat," I said. "Wayne was the founder of Second Chance. I've known him for about a year, and I've done volunteer work for him. Off and on for about twelve months."

Sack sniffed. "Big of you."

I didn't like the comment but chose not to respond. Bay City had for decades been a haven for the homeless, maybe not as much as Skid Row in downtown L.A., but it was a problem nevertheless. My involvement with the Center started innocently enough. Last year I had read that Wayne and Rusty Haas would be making presentations about Second Chance, and I stopped by to speak with Rusty. I had always felt a little bad about what happened to him when we played Notre Dame many years ago. He listened to my apology but offered nothing in the way of forgiveness. Wayne was nearby and struck up a conversation, and the next thing I knew I was being asked to take part in their organization. As Burnside Investigations had seen a dip in business last year, the firm's owner and star employee agreed to be a part of a charitable cause. I had an abundance of spare time after Gail left, and wanted to give a little something back to the community. Get out and meet a few people, improve the world a bit. Sitting at home and brooding was not good for the soul. And Wayne, a born politician, was very effective at persuasion.

"Were you alone when you found the victim?" Sack asked, looking back at his clipboard.

I paused for a moment. "Are you reading these questions off a form?"

The detective looked incredulously at me. "What did you say?"

"I merely inquired whether you were thinking up those questions yourself, or if you found an old copy of Dick Tracy's Crimestopper textbook."

Sack stepped forward and put his face up near mine. He pointed a finger and tried to look menacing.

"You think this is a game?" he asked, and then continued on without waiting for a reply. "Well it ain't. Quit mouthing off or you're going to spend some time in the hoosegow. Clear?"

I paused for a moment to see if he was planning on answering that question too. Since I had been let go from the LAPD three years ago, cops were not my favorite group of people.

"Clear," I finally responded. "Like an azure sky in deepest summer."

Sack's eyes widened but discretion quickly took over. He glanced at the crowd of people milling about, probably remembering that some of them were reporters. Nobody likes a cop with a short fuse, except maybe in the movies.

"Just let me do the intake," Sack said wearily and stepped back. "Again. Were you alone when you found him?"

"All alone."

"Why did you go upstairs?"

"Well, it's like this. Whenever I hear a gunshot I believe it's my civic duty to investigate. It's just in my blood."

"It may get you killed one day," he said, peering at me. "You ever do Security work?"

"Thirteen years on the force. LAPD."

A look of pain came over Sack's face. "You were on the job? What the hell are you giving me such a hard time for then? You know the routine! Why make our lives difficult?"

I grinned at him. "Nothing personal against you. Let's just say I've developed an attitude problem."

"You were dismissed," he guessed.

"That's putting it delicately. I have a history that would straighten your hair."

Sack wiped his face with his fat hand and then looked down at the palm to see how much sweat had accumulated. He flung some moisture to the floor and turned back to his clipboard.

"Who's this Nina Lovejoy?" he asked.

"Volunteer with the Center. She's only been with Second Chance for about a month."

"She sure left her card in an interesting place," he chuckled sarcastically.

"Come on Sack. She's about as likely a suspect as Mother Theresa. I know she did go upstairs with Wayne, sure, but still...."

"Can you say for certain that she the last person you saw with Fairborn?"

I stared at him. "Yes. But you don't actually think Nina was involved?"

"Well, I think maybe she's using a little reverse psychology here. Folks see her go upstairs with the deceased, so she knows she'll be considered a suspect. Drop her card on the victim to make us doubt her. People can surprise you. I've seen it all, believe me."

I blinked a few times. "The old reverse psychology trick," I managed. "I guess they have to get up pretty early in the morning to fool you, Sack."

"Damned early," he said with a measure of pride. "Why

don't we see if we can finish this up quickly, eh? I got a lot of people to talk to."

Finally I agreed with him on something. "Me too," I replied.

*

Sack took my contact information and instructed me not to leave town without telling him. This would hardly pose a problem. I not only didn't have enough money to take a vacation, but I would barely meet my office rent this month.

The police continued their investigation and I began mine. No one was paying me and the police would undoubtedly prefer I stay out of their way. There were a couple of problems with that, though. Wayne Fairborn was a friend, but more importantly he was a friend with a problem and had solicited my help. To find out who killed him, I would first have to learn why he needed me in the first place. No one was paying me, but aside from trailing the dermatologist's wife through a cornucopia of shopping malls, I didn't have much else to fill my days.

In addition to Wayne and I, there had been three people at the workshop tonight who had previously done volunteer work at Second Chance. There was Nina Lovejoy, her boyfriend Mel, and Wayne's brother-in-law, Rusty Haas. As best I could remember, none were downstairs when the shooting occurred. And none were around when the smoke had cleared.

I tried to talk with some of the new volunteers, but after Sack took notice he directed a couple of the uniformed officers to usher me out of the building. As I was escorted into the street, I noticed someone else following us. From his bulky physique, I wondered if Sack hadn't directed one of his goons to work me over. My stomach tensed as he drew near.

"Hey, got a minute?" he asked, as the uniforms trudged past him and walked back inside.

"That depends," I said warily. "What are you selling?"

The big man shook his head, his jowls jiggling ever so slightly. "Not selling anything. Just want to talk."

"That's usually my line. Who are you?"

He gave me a business card with the emblem of the Bay City Tribune on it. "I'm a reporter. Name's Virgil Hairston."

"There used to be a basketball player on the Lakers named Hairston," I remembered. "His nickname was Happy."

"No relation," he said, sticking out his hand. "If there was, I got the fat genes, he got the tall ones."

I shook the hand and put his card in my pocket. "I'm Burnside. I'm a friend of Wayne Fairborn. And also a volunteer at the Center."

"And a private dick if my hearing is still working right."

"Investigator. We like to be called private investigators. The word dick seems to have taken on a whole new meaning in the last fifty years."

Hairston smiled a little. "Understood. What's this Second Chance about?"

"It's a Center designed to help the homeless. It's not a soup kitchen like the one they have near City Hall. It's more of a Placement Center to teach people how to get jobs and support themselves. We give them a helping hand, get them a room somewhere, but it's ultimately up to them to make a life for themselves."

"Sounds like a worthwhile program. Lord knows there are enough homeless around. Think it'll get all these people off the streets?"

"No," I said, shaking my head. "Some are too far gone. This place helps people who can still function in mainstream society."

"What do we do with the rest?" he asked.

"Damn good question."

Hairston jotted something in a notebook and looked up at me. "Were you the candidate's bodyguard?"

I shook my head no. "He's only running for mayor of Bay City. I don't think he's in the type of league where bodyguards are required."

"When he's running against a guy like Jim Callison, you don't take risks."

"Meaning?"

"Meaning there's lots at stake here. Rumor has it Callison's pockets are well lined. A fellow gets used to a lifestyle like that, he doesn't want to give it up so easily."

"And Wayne was becoming a threat."

"Big threat. Not only to the Mayor, but to the people supporting him. There are a couple of major commercial developments in the works in Bay City. Nothing's been approved yet so the business community is, well, concerned."

"You got any ideas yet?" I asked.

"I was hoping you might," he smiled.

"Let's keep in touch," I said, and handed him my card.

He nodded and went back inside and I walked over to my Nissan Pathfinder. It was dark and quiet out as I climbed behind the wheel. I felt a shudder go through my body. The thought of Wayne sitting there lifeless in his chair was enough to make me want to stop at the nearest bar. But drowning my sorrows could wait. There was some business to attend to.

The soft September wind rustled through the tall eucalyptus trees as I drove through the darkened bayside streets. The setting seemed more like small town Peyton Place than suburban Los Angeles. Bay City, a beach community just adjacent to Los Angeles, was strange that way. Some parts of it had the calm serenity of a charming, picturesque burg; other sections had the loud cacophony of a pulsating urban city.

Nina Lovejoy lived in a condominium complex in an upscale part of town, north of Wilshire. There was a security gate, and tall, strapping pines bordered a winding path between the white buildings. I followed a resident in through the gate, and after a few minutes navigated my way to her unit. The bell chimed three times after a single push.

I heard Nina approach, but then there was a silent pause as she most likely glanced through the peephole before opening the door.

"Burnside," she said, a tinge of trepidation edging out of her voice.

"Sorry I'm stopping by so late. You left the Center quickly this evening."

Her orange miniskirt had been replaced by a scarlet t-shirt and powder blue jeans that could have been painted on. She still had on makeup, but would probably look good without it. This woman was clearly a treat for the eyes.

"Would you like to come in?"

I entered the living room, a small, tastefully decorated area with broadloom carpeting, recessed lighting, and a number of brightly colored paintings. I sat down on a director's chair that looked far more comfortable than it actually was.

"Is something wrong?" she asked. "You look very strange."

"You haven't heard?" I countered, eyeing her carefully.

She shook her head no. The movement seemed genuine, but my new buddy Sack had been right about one thing. People can indeed fool you.

I took a deep breath, as much for drama as for strength. "Wayne Fairborn was killed tonight. Someone shot him to death."

She looked at me blankly. "Wayne? Are you serious?"

"Yes."

She shook her head slowly. "There must be some mistake. I was just with him."

"No mistake," I said in a somber voice. "Wayne is dead. He was shot in his office."

The eyes grew huge, and I saw shock beginning to set in. The large china blue eyes began to water. Her full, sensuous lips parted. She blinked a few times, and the tears trickled down her cheeks.

"Wayne?" she repeated. "That can't be true."

"I'm sorry."

"Oh my. Oh my, no. No! NO!"

She dropped her face into her hands and sobbed without restraint. Her long hair fell in front of her face and when she gave a big sniffle, she flung it back violently. She wiped her face with her hands, grabbed a few tissues and rubbed her eyes and her cheeks. Her breath came in spurts. When she turned back to me, her face held a child-like vulnerability, a clean purity you only see in a person when their defenses have been stripped away.

"This is horrible," she sobbed. "I was just with him less than a few hours ago. Who could have done something like that?"

"We don't know yet, Nina. The police are going to come by and ask you what happened. Remember, you don't have to talk to them. You have the right to an attorney."

"What are you saying? I didn't have anything to do with... oh, you can't mean..."

"They think you're a suspect."

"That's crazy," she cried. "How could anyone think that?"

I pulled out my address book and wrote down the phone number of an excellent criminal defense attorney.

"Call this man tonight," I said, "and do whatever he tells you to do. From everything I've seen, you have at least someone convinced you didn't do it."

"Thank you," she said. "That helps."

I nodded. Sometimes a brevity of words can speak volumes. I left without saying anything more.

Three

I awoke at five the next morning to the sound of a bed creaking violently. Disdaining alarm clocks, my nocturnal slumber was normally disrupted by either a homeless person digging through the garbage cans outside my window or by an overactive libido. About twice a week my downstairs neighbor, Ms. Linzmeier, would engage in some horizontal exercise with a boyfriend who apparently had little use for sleep. I considered pounding on the floor but decided they were too focused to hear anything. Instead I listened and thought of Gail Pepper, and a maudlin feeling of loneliness swept over me. We had met last year, and she quickly became an integral part of my life. I missed Gail tremendously, and though Berkeley was just up the coast, it seemed a million miles away. I took a hot shower and tried to forget the pain in my soul for a while.

It was still dark when I fixed three cups of French roast coffee and sat at my desk to read the online fish wrap, also known as the website for L.A.'s premier daily newspaper. Good coffee was one of the pleasures I afforded myself, regardless of whatever financial circumstances I happened to be in. The one I was mired in now was not pretty. But some habits simply become part of your life, and the cost of a good pot of coffee was relatively small. I wasn't ready to shelve everything because of a small detail like insolvency.

The L.A. Times story on Wayne was buried in the second section and was brief. Far more space was devoted to USC's football team which had won its first three games, and would now begin conference play. The weather would be the same all week, high of 74, low of 55. As I finished combing through the news, a queasy feeling came over me. I had committed a *faux pas* last night by interfering with a police investigation. If Sack found out, he could easily collar me and make my life profoundly miserable. And if Nina Lovejoy had actually committed the shooting, I could be charged with aiding and abetting a murderer. Taking my license away would merely be a prelude for harsher things to come.

When a person reaches a certain age though, they learn to trust their instincts. Gut feeling becomes part of the process. I had been in law enforcement for over sixteen years and had cultivated what I believed to be a keen eye for when someone was being straight with me. My gut had only failed me once, and that misstep had cost me my badge. If it failed me this time I stood to lose a good bit more. Without my P.I. license I might spend the rest of my days wearing a rent-a-cop uniform and snoozing at a security desk. But I'd bet the ranch that Nina Lovejoy had nothing to do with Wayne's murder. Only a small part of me harbored any doubt.

Not being acquainted with many officers at the Bay City Police Department, and not having impressed many last night, I concluded that paying them a visit now would hardly serve my better interests. I had a very casual acquaintance with a uniform named Carl O'Brien who played in my softball league, but decided to save that one for another occasion. His nickname was Ox and if he performed police work like he played catcher, he would be a good guy to have on my side.

I skipped breakfast and decided to take a drive into the South Bay to begin talking with a few people who were at Second Chance last night. As I headed down the crowded San Diego freeway, I felt as if I were driving within the confines of a misty cloud, the color of a soiled shirt collar. The smog had been exceptionally thick the past few days, the local meteorologists claiming an inversion layer was trapping warm air within the foothills that surrounded the Los Angeles basin. Technically they were mountains, but anyone who had driven through Colorado or Utah found that laughable. These large foothills created abominable temperatures in the local valleys and often prevented the cool ocean breezes from keeping the southland ventilated. September was the worst month of the year for smog, and thankfully it was almost over.

The address I had listed for Rusty and Sara Haas was on Emerald Street in Redondo Beach. It was a small house, painted light blue, and sat on a little hill across the street from a park. The interior probably held less square feet than my apartment, but was undoubtedly worth in excess of half a million dollars. As they say, location is everything.

I rang the bell, and a sleepy looking guy wearing a purple and gold Lakers t-shirt opened the door. He mumbled hello and tried to blink some daylight into his eyes.

"Hi there," I said loudly, flashing a gold badge that read "Private Investigations" in flashy blue lettering. "Name's Burnside. I'm conducting an inquiry. Can I see some identification?"

"Whaaaa..? What's going on?" he stuttered.

This was going to be fun. "Do you live here, son?" I asked.

"Nnnn-no, no I don't," he said as he fished through his pockets for his wallet. I raised my eyebrows noticeably and he quickly continued. "I'm supposed to be here. My brother just bought this place."

"I can verify that, you know."

"Uh-huh," he said, finally digging a crumpled driver's license out and handing it over to me. The name on it read "Alan Ulrich." He was twenty-two years old.

"What happened to the Haas family?" I asked in my most suspicious voice.

"They moved."

"Know where?"

He frowned and walked off into the kitchen. After a few minutes I wondered if he had gone back to sleep. Miraculously he did come back to the door, and he carried a slip of paper in his hand.

"They just moved this weekend," he said. "Are they in some kind of trouble?"

"We don't know yet," I said in a heavy handed voice and then peered at him. "If I need to speak to your brother, where can I find him?"

"He'll be back tonight. He's on the road all day. Salesman, you know."

"Yeah, I know," I said, handing him back his driver's license, I thanked him curtly for the address and quickly walked off. One thing was certain. Alan Ulrich was wide awake by now.

I headed east along Torrance Boulevard through a neighborhood of simple, stucco houses, with an occasional fast food joint on a corner. The Haas address was along a stretch known as the City Strip. It was a narrow, ten mile sliver of land that extended the city of Los Angeles' confines southward from Watts towards San Pedro. By maintaining an unbroken boundary through the South Bay, the city was able to have a direct path to the lucrative harbor. Some of the residents of the City Strip were not even aware they lived in Los Angeles. Many thought they were in a part of Torrance or Gardena. They often found out the hard way, usually when they needed police assistance and the nearest LAPD patrol car was miles away. And not anxious to fight traffic to get to them.

I parked near a sodden apartment building featuring pale green paint that was chipping, and numbers on the front that were badly faded. A few children played in the front courtyard and their mothers jabbered away nearby. I climbed a flight of stairs and walked across the outdoor passageway to apartment "J". I pushed the doorbell and heard no buzzer go off. No one responded. In this building, knocking proved far more effective.

The door opened and Rusty Haas stood there giving me a surprised look. Rusty was a beefy six-two and probably weighed two-fifty. He was wearing a t-shirt, sweat pants, and sneakers with small cleats on them. Rusty had a shaved head that masked his male pattern baldness, and he sported a ginger colored goatee. Some people may have thought that to be trendy, but on Rusty it just made him look like he had a dirty face. His clothing hung from his body like laundry on a clothesline.

"Burnside?" he said in a quizzical manner. "What brings you down here?"

"Can I come in?" I asked.

Rusty hesitated for a second and then stepped back from the door. "It's a little messy," he said. "We're just getting settled."

"Not for very long," came a female voice from the next room. Sara Haas walked out in similar attire as her husband. "This is just a way station for us."

I looked around the living room at some very elegant furniture surrounded by boxes full of books and clothes and kitchenware. Framed photos of family members, distant beaches, and Rusty in his blue and gold Notre Dame uniform were scattered along the floor. Some tennis rackets, fishing rods, and a pair of red Sports World gym bags were piled in a corner.

"It's a far cry from the beach house you moved from," I commented wryly.

"I know," she said, "but with Rusty getting laid off, it was too hard to make the mortgage payments on one income. We needed a place and this was the first thing we found. We won't be here long. Just until we get back on our feet."

"What do you do for a living?" I asked Sara.

"I used to be a teacher, that's how Rusty and I met. Now I'm a writer."

"What do you write about?"

She shrugged. "Oh, anything and everything. Social issues. Balancing career and relationships. When to marry, who to marry. Navigating through a changing world. Modern life, you might say."

The two of them stood side by side. They were a couple of years younger than I was, but I thought they looked a good bit older. Sara's light brown hair fell down past her shoulders and was beginning to have strands of grey. Unlike her younger sister Crystal, she had lost that sensuousness of youth, even though she was just as slender. Rusty and Sara looked decidedly middle aged, Rusty having added about thirty pounds since his days as a fullback with Notre Dame. His main job back then had been to block for the tailbacks, but when he got an opportunity to carry the ball he was a load to bring down. I was two years ahead of Rusty but only played against him once, on a cloudy October day in South Bend. USC came away the victor, and it was a game both of us would remember for the rest of our lives.

"Have you heard about what happened to Wayne last night?"

Rusty sighed and nodded. "The cops called us last night. We have to go in and speak with them this morning."

"How's Crystal taking it?"

Sara spoke. "Not well. The police were over at my sister's house last night. Poor thing. Crystal's had to deal with a lot. This was just a tremendous shock. I heard about it on the radio last night, driving home. I nearly crashed the Mustang. I didn't get any sleep at all last night."

I waited and said nothing. An awkward silence ensued.

Rusty sighed. "It's funny how someone is alive one minute and gone the next."

"It usually works that way," I muttered dryly, and turned to Sara. "Did you visit Crystal last night?"

"No," she said. "Dad went up to be with her. And he was very angry with the way the police were investigating."

"Did Crystal ever mention anyone with whom she and Wayne might have had problems?" I asked perfunctorily.

"What do you mean she and Wayne?" Sara asked. "Crystal didn't have an enemy in the world. She's the warmest person you could ever find!"

"Warm or not, somebody tried to run her off the road the other night. Wayne told me about it. He didn't think it was an accident."

They looked at each other blankly and shrugged.

Sara spoke. "If you're looking for a motive, you don't have to go beyond his family. Peter's resented Wayne for years."

"Peter?" I asked.

"Wayne's brother," she said, with a slight amount of distaste. "Our brother-in-law. We don't talk about him much. He's a bum and a low life. He lives over in Hermosa Beach, spends his days playing volleyball and his nights drinking beer in some hole-in-the-wall pub."

"Doesn't sound like the type of guy who'd want to commit murder, does it?" I asked, playing devil's advocate.

"It does when he's cut out of daddy's will," Rusty said. "When the estate is worth over a hundred million dollars. That could send someone off the deep end in a big way."

"Could be," I said, and took down Peter's address. I decided to pursue another tact. "Rusty, did you see anything unusual at the Center last night. Something that caught your eye as different?"

Rusty frowned and looked up at the ceiling. "Last night," he managed. "I think I noticed one of the janitors going upstairs. When I took the podium I had a partial view of the stairwell and saw one of them leave the room. I thought it was odd, too. Most of their work up there was finished for the night."

"Anything else?"

Rusty shook his head slowly. "Nothing. Like I said, I left right after the orientation was done."

I nodded. "How did you and Wayne get along?"

"Wait a minute," Sara broke in, pointing a finger at me as her face reddened. "Are you making an accusation here?"

"It sounded more like a question, wouldn't you say?"

"I'd say you're not a police officer," she said defiantly. "And I personally resent this interrogation."

"It's not an interrogation. And he's going to get questioned eventually by the police," I said. "This way he can get his story straight."

Rusty's face turned into a snarl and he grabbed my collar and yanked hard. He asked who the hell I thought I was, and before I could answer he shoved me up against a wall. We strained against each other for a minute until I felt pressure on my windpipe. Breathing became difficult. I tried to slam my forearm into his to break the grip, but his arm barely moved. Needle-like pains shot up my wrist and stung mercilessly.

With desperation rising, I grabbed his thumb with my right hand and bent it backwards. As his grip loosened, I ducked under his arm, twisting it behind his back in one motion, and jerking it upward in a hammer lock. I jerked it again, harder this time. He grunted at the pain and started hollering for me to let go. I felt the air move haltingly in and out of my throat.

"Don't mess with me," I whispered hoarsely. "You're an out of shape ex-jock. I work out five times a week and I'm better at defense than you are at offense. That's something you should have learned twenty years ago."

With that I released the pressure and he stared at me angrily, rubbing his wrist. I found myself doing the same thing.

"You've got a lot of nerve coming here, Burnside," he said glaring harshly at me. "Why don't you take your stupid ideas somewhere else. And I haven't forgotten what you did a long time ago."

*

Peter Fairborn wasn't at his beach apartment so I drove back to Bay City. I had put my cell phone on vibrate, so I noticed I had had two calls, one from Virgil Hairston of the Tribune and one from my only paying client, the dermatologist with the supposedly wayward wife. Both callers were unavailable when I phoned them back.

Having finally developed an appetite, I went over to a vegan restaurant on San Vicente that a healthy looking client had once raved about. I wolfed down a burrito stuffed with tofu, black beans, quinoa and grilled vegetables, and decided the concept was more satisfying than the execution. My client might have had enhanced levels of pulchritude, but decidedly under-developed taste buds.

I climbed back into my black Pathfinder and drove over to Second Chance. The Center was headquartered along Pico Boulevard in a seedier part of Bay City, and it was distinguished by being the only building on the street to have a fresh coat of paint. A massage parlor was located across the street, along with a couple of sleazy bars, a laundromat and a rundown liquor store. Wayne could have afforded nicer digs but in this arena you set up shop where the market is.

There were a number of raggedy looking people milling about the entrance, and I gave the palms up sign when one of them asked if I had any spare change. In addition to going against the spirit of Second Chance, I was in no position to hand money away. Advice and encouragement were the best I could offer these days.

Inside, the office was hectic to say the least. A long strip of bright yellow police tape blocked off the entrance to Wayne's office and various chalk lines and powders draped the interior. For a moment I thought I saw a vision of Wayne sitting amidst the bedlam, looking around in confusion. I closed my eyes. Wayne was dead and it was going to take some time to get used to it.

Jerry Winkler was finishing up a phone conversation as I darkened his desk. He concluded by telling the other party to hang in there and not get depressed. Words to live by.

"I see that life goes on."

Jerry nodded definitively. "We're still open for business. Crystal indicated she wanted to keep it going. In memory of Wayne and all. You'll notice the homeless problem is still with us."

"First hand. Have you spoken with the police?"

"The police, the media, the volunteers, you name it. The cops said they'd be back later on to finish up. Whatever that means. Don't touch anything, I suppose. All I know is this place is a holy mess."

"Say Jerry, could you get a couple of addresses for me? I need to get in touch with the guys you hired in as janitors. Also, that fellow Nina hangs around with, Mel something-or-other?"

Jerry sighed and pulled open a rolodex. "I should be getting used to this. The police have practically made me the center post of their operation. Addresses, phone numbers, who's friends with who. I never realized what a veritable gold mine of information the director of this Center is."

Patting him on the shoulder, I left and drove over to Wayfarer Hotel in Venice. This was the flop house where Eddy and Raff both lived, but neither were in their rooms. My inquiry as to when they might return was met with a blank look by the front desk girl; her only task seemed to be chewing her gum methodically. I pulled out my phone and called Virgil Hairston again. This time I was more successful.

"Burnside," he shouted at me, "I've been trying to catch you all day. I want to get your opinion on what's happened."

"I'm a slippery devil. What's up?"

"You don't know?"

"Trust me. I'm as in the dark as one can be right now."

"The police now have a suspect in custody. Nice looking, if my sources are accurate."

I took a deep breath. Hopefully Nina Lovejoy heeded my advice and called the attorney.

"When did they pick her up?"

"This morning. In an hour or so you can read all about it."

"You guys don't miss a beat," I said.

"Hey, it's big news when a political candidate is shot. It's even bigger news when it's the guy's wife that's the suspect. Isn't that an interesting turn of events?"

My mouth was agape. Interesting indeed.

Four

The Tribune building was located along a stretch of Colorado Avenue that was equal parts industrial, commercial, and residential. Back in the days when zoning was merely a gleam in someone's eye, erecting an office building or a factory next to a row of houses was an occasional if not common practice. Tough luck for the homeowner.

The paper's offices were minimalist to say the least. Muted orange carpeting, cut into eighteen-inch squares, were stitched together along the floor and the desks held some of the cheapest looking metal accessories this side of an army base. Only a municipal agency's digs could rival this. I found Virgil Hairston's cubicle easily enough, as a sportswriter told me to follow the pungent aroma. Sure enough, sitting behind a box of take out fried chicken was the crime reporter himself.

"Early dinner?"

"This is just a snack," he said, tearing into a crusty drumstick. He pushed the greasy-looking box towards me. "Have some."

I was indeed a little hungry but my discerning palate was not about to cave. Ben & Jerry's ice cream was worth veering off of an otherwise healthy diet. So was a pastrami sandwich from Langer's. But certain limits needed to be drawn. I'd settle for a rumbling stomach.

"So the police have cracked the case," I remarked.

"You sound as if you have some doubts," he answered as he gnawed away at the drumstick.

"I doubt everything," I said. "Give me an update."

"The police found a witness."

"Who?"

"Some girl named Amy Flanders, a volunteer at the Center. She says Fairborn's wife walked out the back door of the building. Saw a few other people leave through that way also, but she claims the wife was there."

"Crystal denying it?"

"Implicitly. Her alibi was that she was home alone the whole evening, so obviously there were no witnesses. Also, the police checked out her car. Dried blood stains all over her steering wheel, the seat, you name it. They also found out Wayne owned a .32 pistol, same caliber as the murder weapon. Not surprisingly, that's gone."

I frowned. "That doesn't sound like enough to press charges."

"Maybe not," he said. "But her old man got out of line and the cops tossed them both in the tank. Seems he became a bit indignant when they implied she might have some reason to kill her husband. Took a swing at one of the uniforms."

I looked across Hairston's desk and noticed the splash page of the paper's website on his computer. The headline blared, "Wife Held in Fairborn Murder!" I shook my head and turned back to watch the big man finish the last of his snack.

"The police do jump to conclusions," I said, my bitterness perhaps showing more than I had intended.

"Oh?" he chuckled in a reporter's cynical way. "You don't doubt our men in blue, do you?"

"I've known too many of them. Some are good, some are not. But I've known Crystal for a while. It would take a lot for her to shoot anybody, much less her husband. It's not implausible, but something doesn't smell right."

"You must have been a good cop once."

"A lifetime ago."

Hairston wiped his hands carefully with a paper napkin and turned back to business. "Okay Burnside. Let's say it wasn't the wife. Who could it have been?"

"The question of the day," I said. "A criminal attorney might disagree with this, but from my point of view there are two basic types of murders. Those committed in the heat of the moment and those that are premeditated. Most are the former, but from a premeditated standpoint a political assassination can't be ruled out. On that score, Wayne was involved in a tight campaign with Callison. The Mayor had a lot to lose. So did his big supporters."

"Real estate interests, I presume."

"Maybe," I said. "Probably. Finding out who his big donors are is a first step."

"I can help with that," Hairston said, jotting a note down onto a pad of yellow legal paper. "Also, if someone had a personal vendetta against Fairborn, that would be a possibility."

"Sure," I agreed. "But this wasn't a guy many people disliked. Politicians get ahead by ingratiating themselves to everybody. Making too many enemies can shorten a career."

"So that brings us to crimes committed in the heat of the moment."

"Right. If we explore that path, someone saw Wayne

committing an act that maybe offended or horrified them enough to make him pay the ultimate price."

"Okay," Hairston pondered. "So he went upstairs with this hot blonde. That could have sent his wife off the deep end."

"If she were there."

"Or someone that respected Wayne and maybe had that respect, trust, whatever, betrayed."

"Or," I added, "someone that cared about Nina. A boyfriend, perhaps."

Hairston nodded. "Women that look like Nina always seem to have boyfriends," he said. "Whether they want them or not."

"That's a bit sexist, Virgil," I said, smiling at him.

"It's true," he shrugged.

I kept smiling without taking a stand on the issue. Politics wasn't hard, I thought. The job amounted to simply not saying the wrong things. Or at least giving yourself room to wiggle.

"There's one other possible scenario we haven't explored," I pointed out. "Killing out of fear."

"Fear? Like being trapped?"

"In a way. If Wayne caught somebody doing something they weren't supposed to, that person might have panicked and shot him. If they had time to think about it, pulling the trigger might seem ludicrous, but they might not have had the time to think."

"Like surprising a burglar in your home?"

A light bulb went on over my head. "Exactly."

"So let me see if I've got it. Your experience is that people kill due to one of a few basic motivations. Anger, fear or jealousy."

I thought back to my conversation with Wayne the night before and shivered.

"Maybe all three," I said softly.

*

It was nearly nine o'clock by the time I pulled in front of the Wayfarer Hotel in Venice. A few people out front eyed my Pathfinder with curiosity. I made a big production out of activating the alarm with the remote switch on my key chain, sending two piercing beeps into the air and making the headlights flash twice.

The gum-cracking day clerk was replaced by an elderly man wearing a grayish green sweater and a nylon golf shirt buttoned to the top. A visor that advertised Lucky Strikes adorned his head. Next to the desk was a sofa that had seen better days, and a pair of rickety folding chairs. The filthy carpeting had cigarette butts sprinkled liberally about. I looked around at the seedy lounge and wondered how low a person had to fall before he hit this level. Or if there was anything lower, besides the gutter.

"Help you?" the man asked, in a gravelly voice that had probably been eaten away by too much cheap wine.

"I'm looking for a guy named Raff. What room is he in?"

"Raff?" he peered at me, scratching his head. "I can't remember no Raff."

I sighed and pushed a five dollar bill at him. "Put your thinking cap on."

He snatched the bill eagerly and pocketed it. "Room six," he said. "Go down the hall to your right."

The hallway was dark, which served the purpose of masking the hideous surroundings from my view. But nothing could hide the sharp, acrid odor that filled my nostrils. A radio blaring hip hop music was audible from outside of room six. It was turned down immediately when I rapped loudly on the door.

"All right, all right. I'll keep it down!"

I frowned and rapped again, softer this time. The door opened a minute later and a hard looking man wearing jeans, a black shirt and a pair of black framed glasses, opened the door. "Yes?"

"Hi Raff. How are you?"

He squinted at me for a moment before recognition swept across his face. A smile didn't follow it.

"Yes. I remember you. The fellow from the Center."

"Right. Name's Burnside. We met at a workshop a few weeks ago."

"Yes. A few weeks ago," he said, still squinting at me.

"Uh, Raff, I need to talk with you for a minute. Can I come in?"

He looked back into the room at his belongings strewn about the floor. Clothes, towels, books, newspapers and boxes were spread haphazardly here and there. Finally deciding it wasn't too atrocious, he motioned me inside.

"I'm sorry for the appearance. I have not had the time lately for cleaning."

I held up my palms. "A man should not be judged by the amount of clutter on his floor."

He tilted his head. "Confucius?"

I shook my head and smiled. "More like Oscar Madison."

The squinting continued. "I've never read his work," he admitted.

"Few have," I said.

Raff took off his spectacles and rubbed his eyes. "These are my new glasses. I suppose the prescription isn't exact. Not that I really need them now for the work I do as a janitor. It's not what I've been training for."

"I heard you were a student."

"At UCLA. I was in the PhD program. Political Science was my field, Methods to be exact. I was doing my dissertation on the shrinking middle class. I had no idea I would get a practical lesson in that subject, but a few months ago my fellowship was discontinued. Not enough money I was told. Without the funding I could not continue my studies. Nor could I keep my apartment."

"I understand. It's happened to a lot of people, but at least you're trying to get your life together. You're a bright guy. What happened to you could have happened to anyone. You'll find another path soon."

"Of course," he said bitterly. "Perhaps one day I can supervise janitors. Earn enough to afford an apartment in a better slum than this. While the rich get richer."

I nodded sympathetically and lifted a couple of books from a desk chair to sit down. "Raff, I'm a private investigator. I need to ask you a few questions."

His face tightened and his lips scrunched up. I looked at his hands and they were balled up into fists. This was clearly a candidate for a stress management seminar.

"I don't have to answer anything without an attorney present," he said. "I know my rights."

"Yes, I imagine you do. But let me assure you, I'm not a police officer. If you haven't done anything wrong, you have no reason to worry. Did you hear what happened at the Center last night?"

"There was an orientation meeting."

"After the meeting."

"I don't know anything."

I paused. "Wayne Fairborn, the Center's founder, was shot to death last night. Did you know that?"

"I do not know anything about a shooting," he said in a mechanical way. "Not one thing."

"An eyewitness says you left the premises before the orientation ended. That would put you in the clear, wouldn't it?"

He froze for a moment. "Yes," he finally said. "Yes, it certainly would."

I tried a new tact. "Another eyewitness said they saw you upstairs at the time of the shooting."

"That is a complete lie," he retorted, although his eyes were fixed someplace other than on mine. The muscles in his face tightened.

"You know Raff, a person's been murdered. You may have seen something, heard something perhaps. Nobody's accusing you, but it would help me inordinately if you remembered anything about last night. Anything at all."

For a moment my eyes locked onto his, but it was only for a moment. As he diverted his eyes again I looked around the room at the mess that could rival any teenager's. I caught a glimpse of something out of place. On a small desk across the room, atop a pile of books, was a shiny silver pen stand. The chrome base was elegantly curved, and two long cylinders holding silver pens were sticking up at forty-five degree angles. I rose and walked over for a closer look. Engraved in the base were three initials, WJF.

"Nice souvenir," I remarked. "Was this a gift from Mr. Fairborn or do you figure God helps those who help themselves?"

Raff stood up straight and glared at me. "It was a gift."

I laughed and shook my head. "Raff, you don't get it. People don't give away things with their initials carved into them. Also, Wayne was the kind of guy who believed people should earn things. They should get helping hands, not handouts. You swiped this from the Center. My only question is when."

"I think I will have to ask you to leave."

I stood there looking into the hardened face, the cold eyes, the unyielding posture. "I'll leave. But if you're involved in this, I'll find out. And our next meeting may not be so pleasant and carefree."

Raff took a step towards me in a menacing way but I pointed my left index finger at him and drew back my right fist.

"Don't even think about it," I warned him. Looking at my size, he stopped in his tracks. At least his brain wasn't completely atrophied.

"That's the first smart move you've made so far," I remarked, and walked back out into the putrid hallway.

Five

The next morning I was up at my normal six o'clock, as Ms. Linzmeier apparently chose to spend the night alone. The light began to filter through the curtains tepidly, the soft rays stirring me in a delicate manner. I showered and dressed and then scooped some Mocha Java into the coffeemaker. Setting it in motion, I decided to walk over to a local bakery on Montana. Stepping over a sleeping young man sporting a light blond stubble on his face, I picked up a warm loaf of sourdough bread from a cheery woman behind the counter. I asked how long the man had been sleeping in front of the building, but she just shrugged and said he was in the same position when she arrived. She didn't have the heart to wake him. Climbing over him on the way out, I checked to make sure he was still breathing. It was a little difficult to tell, but the occasional rise and fall of his chest told me he was still taking in air. Whether he was truly living or not was an altogether different subject. Not having the heart to wake him either, I moved on down the street, feeling a little more grateful for my own existence, modest as it might be.

After breakfast, I decided to start my day with a local visit. It took about five minutes to reach the Bay City police station, and an hour of waiting for Crystal Fairborn. She was finally brought to the glass enclosed booth typically reserved for attorney-client discussions. We were separated by a glass partition, easily an inch thick, and successful at muffling most sounds. Telephones on either side of the booth were necessary for talking. Even though we were only a few feet away, her voice sounded as if we were separated by an ocean.

"Crystal," I said softly, "how are you holding up?"

She shook her head and said nothing. Looking down, she started to speak but no words came out. She looked miserable, as would one whose world had just collapsed. Tears slid down her cheeks.

"I understand what you're going through," I said slowly. "Maybe I can help. If you're innocent, I can promise you that I'll do whatever's in my power to get you off. But first you have to talk to me."

Her soft grey eyes looked into mine. They were tinged with red and had a pleading look to them. The normally pretty face was now drawn and gaunt. Crystal was in her early thirties, and had ash blonde hair that fell past her shoulders in an elegant manner. A beauty mark sat just to the right of her lower lip. Even in her orange prison garb, she managed to exude a certain ornate refinement.

"You probably can guess," she stammered, "that this is the most horrible time of my life."

"Tell me about what happened," I asked gently.

"Yesterday," she said, her voice almost choking, "the police marched into my home like a group of storm troopers and took over. They assumed I was guilty and were going to pull a confession out of me. Oh, thank God my father was there. At least I had a witness. The police... they were ready to write a confession out and sign it for me."

"I know the feeling."

"Oh, it was awful! I've never been treated so badly. If only Wayne were... oh, he would never have stood for it. This whole thing is a nightmare!"

She began to cry, her eyes closed tightly and her body trembling. Her lower lip protruded and her face revealed the agony of one who was suffering deeply. I waited patiently until she sniffled and began to wipe her face.

"Crystal, let's talk about what happened last week. Wayne told me something about an SUV following you along Sunset?"

She blew her nose and looked up at me with those red, bleary eyes. I felt my own heart strings being pulled.

"I was driving home last week from a function. I don't know how long this truck was in back of me, but once I got onto Sunset they began driving extremely close. Finally, there was a stretch that curved sharply around an embankment and that's when they passed and tried to run me off the road."

"Any damage?"

"A little. There was a dent, and some paint was scraped on my car," she said and held up her left hand that had a gauze bandage applied to the heel. "And I cut my hand on something when we collided."

"Any idea as to who might have done it?"

"Oh, Burnside, I don't know. I've never hurt anyone. And if someone were after Wayne, why would they try to harm me? How would that help anything?"

"They might have been trying to send him a message. Or scare him into doing something. Do you know anything about this?"

She steadied her eyes downward. "He had received some threatening phone calls. They would just say that Wayne better do the right thing, but he never told me what that right thing was."

"Man or a woman?"

"He couldn't tell. They would disguise their voice for gosh sake! And they would always speak to him, they'd hang up when I'd answer. Oh, this whole thing... it's just too horrible for words! Burnside, you've got to help me! Please!"

"I'll do what I can," I said grimly. "One last thing. You didn't go to Second Chance the night Wayne was shot?"

She shook her head no.

"Do you know a woman named Amy Flanders?"

Crystal's eyes turned hard. "Yes," she said. "Why?"

"Amy was the one who identified you as walking out of the alley behind the Center right after the shooting."

A wave of horror spread across her face and her mouth hung open. "That woman is unbelievable," she started. "She is just a complete monster."

"How well do you know her?"

"I... I can't talk about it. I simply can't," she said.

"All right," I said, knowing this wouldn't be the right time to probe.

"It's just too difficult."

I saw the jailor check her watch and start to move towards us. I remembered something else. "This may be unrelated, but do you know if Wayne gave away a pen stand to one of the homeless?"

Crystal shook her head blankly. "I don't know. I don't know anything about that."

Before I could follow up with anything else, the khaki jailor was next to us, saying our time was up. I stood and watched as Crystal was led back to her cell, her tear stained face the picture of injustice. She had just lost her husband and was now suspected of having killed him. The two worst things in the world had just happened to her.

*

I spent the bulk of the afternoon reacquainting myself with the dermatologist's wife, Violet, and following her from one trendy Westside boutique to another. Why Doctor Leary hired my services was beyond me, as there wasn't even the hint of infidelity. From my vantage point, her biggest sin was spending money like a drunken sailor. At five-thirty she ended her taxing workday.

In the three years since I formed my investigations agency, I always had the luxury of an office. There were a few times when the cash flow was mostly a one way operation, but something always materialized and I made the nut. Good thing for me because I dreaded the thought of working out of my apartment. Not only does it make a poor impression on potential clients, but cabin fever is a real issue when business is slow.

I had received one call during the afternoon from Mel Fenster, one of the volunteers who had been at Second Chance the other night. Mel said he would be at his store until closing, which meant I could call until eleven. He probably meant call by phone but I was big on seeing a person's reactions when I quizzed them.

I parked along Pico Boulevard just past Cloverdale, in front of a sign that read "Fenster & Son, Liquor and Jr.

Market". The lights were on and the son sat on a stool at the cash register, reading a magazine. As I walked towards the entrance I noticed two indigents setting up their campsite along the sidewalk. They had unrolled blankets and were using a pile of clothes as pillows. A chrome shopping cart stuffed with various belongings was positioned just a few feet away, their possessions stowed away in rumpled, white plastic trash bags.

I entered the store and the jingling of bells signaled that the door had been opened. Mel looked up suspiciously before he recognized who it was.

"Mr. Burnside," he said. "I thought you'd phone first."

Mel Fenster was in his early thirties, a lanky man with long black hair. He had an olive complexion, enhanced undoubtedly by plenty of hours laying out on the local beaches. Bay City had no shortage of lovely shoreline, but the water was sometimes unfit to swim in because of repeated sewage spills from a local treatment plant. It was a pathetic irony. We live in paradise, we just can't enjoy it.

"It's a nasty habit of mine," I replied. "Besides, in my line of work people with good manners rarely excel at their job."

The store was divided into four sections, a huge magazine rack, a pitifully small area that held some food and household items, a cooler that mostly contained beer and soda, and a vast liquor wall behind the counter. Bright lights emanated from a series of long incandescent tubes, and the floors were slick and shiny.

"I read that article about Crystal in the Tribune earlier today," he said, closing the magazine he was reading. "What a story, huh?"

I looked down at his magazine. The latest issue of GQ. The cover story was why men who shaved their body hair made better lovers.

"Don't believe everything you read," I cautioned and looked up at him.

"Really? You think someone besides Crystal did it?"

I paused to re-focus on the topic at hand. "Uh-huh. I don't think this case is closed. Not by a long shot."

"Don't I know it," he scoffed. "I have, like, no use for the cops around here. The ones at the Center kept us till almost one a.m. the other night."

"What did they ask you?"

"Oh, you know. What I saw, who I saw, when I saw it. What I knew about Wayne. The whole deal."

"Just what did you see?" I asked.

He shrugged. "Not too much. Nina told me she went upstairs for a minute with Wayne. I guess she was doing an article about California politics for that magazine of hers and wanted to interview him. Can you believe the police actually went over to her place and grilled her until the middle of the night? These guys act like we don't have lives of our own. If I were there, I'd have tossed 'em out."

"You and Nina still seeing each other?"

"Sure," he said, giving me a sideways look. "We've been together, oh, must be a couple of months now."

"Nice girl."

"Yeah," he said, sliding around on his stool. "A real sweetheart. Of course, I don't let her know that."

"No?"

"Nah," he sneered and gave me an ugly wink. "Gotta keep

babes guessing, let 'em know they're not the only fish in the sea. Keep them off balance. You know."

I knew that if I tried that with Gail Pepper she'd likely take a swing at me. I waited for him to continue.

"I'm a little surprised they got his wife in mind as the culprit, though," he said. "That's not the angle I'd look at."

"Who do you suspect?"

"A loser. One of Wayne's clients, or whatever he called them. Hey look, whenever someone like Wayne's made it, there's always a crazy guy out there who thinks he has to even the score. Someone that can't accept life's fate."

As he spoke, the jingling of bells interrupted his stream of words and we watched a man wearing a scuzzy black sweat shirt enter the store. Mel's eyes followed him as the man perused the cooler and came out with a bottle of Coke. Placing it on the counter, he dropped a pile of grubby looking change next to the cash register.

"I'll pay outta that," he wheezed.

"Look buddy, if you can't count, then take off. I don't want your business that bad."

"It's money, ain't it?" he demanded angrily. "You can take it or leave it, but I'm drinking this puppy."

With that, the man twisted open the cap and took a long swig. He glowered up at Mel and asked him if he wanted the Coke back. Mel reached down, hurriedly counted out some change, and pushed the rest back at him.

"Take it and get lost," he sneered. "Do me a favor and go shop at 7-Eleven next time."

The man pocketed what was left over on the counter. "No sir," he declared. "I like it in here. You all are so nice to me, I think I'm gonna tell all my friends about this place."

With the wry smile of a small battle won, the man strutted out of the store. Mel glared as he walked through the glass doors, a cold hostility forming in his eyes.

"Damn homeless," he sneered. "See what I have to put up with? And the police won't do a thing about them. They just keep saying their hands are tied because the Mayor doesn't want to prosecute them. I tell you, pretty soon Bay City's going to look like Skid Row downtown."

"If you feel this way, why volunteer at Second Chance?"

He hesitated for a moment before replying. Judging from the anger still remaining on his face, he seemed to be replaying the scene in his mind. Or replaying a previous encounter.

"Well it's mostly Nina's idea. But I liked the concept Wayne had. Helping people help themselves. Show 'em how to pull themselves up by their own bootstraps. That's the American Way. That's my way."

It sounded good but judging from the Fenster & Son sign on the door, old Mel probably had some help finding his own bootstraps, much less hoisting himself up by them. He did make a point about Second Chance though. There were a variety of shelters on the Westside of Los Angeles that offered services to the homeless. They provided some meals but not a lot more. The Second Chance philosophy was to give people direction rather than handouts. We held clinics on how to get a job, an apartment, and above all how to adjust back into society. It was a tough, no-nonsense approach geared towards getting clients to straighten out their own lives. Wayne felt there were some people we could help, and some who were too far gone.

Turning back to Mel, I asked him if he had any specific idea who might have shot Wayne Fairborn. The icy look remained.

"Like I said," he growled, "I think it was one of those homeless. I tell you, these guys are just plain jealous of us, because we've made it and they haven't. And Wayne's made it big, and they couldn't handle that."

"Go on," I said.

"Personally, I think it was one of those two janitors we hired. Eddy or that weird guy, what's his name?"

"Raff?"

"Yeah, Raff. In fact, I saw Raff hurrying down the street after the workshop was over. Like he couldn't wait to get outta there."

I stiffened. "When?"

"About ten minutes after we finished up. I walked outside for a smoke, it's against people's religion to allow cigarette smoke indoors these days. Raff took off a few minutes later in a major hurry. He had something under his coat, too. Something bulky."

"Did you by any chance see anyone else leave around then?"

"Sure," he whined. "But they were normal folks. Like you and me."

"Did you tell the police this?" I asked.

"The police," he scoffed. "Yeah, I told that cop, Sack. But it was like he didn't even hear me. Went in one ear and out the other. Just like when I ask 'em to get rid of those bums outside my store. They just turn a blind eye. Businessmen like me, we just get squeezed."

I looked around his store, the store his father probably worked like a dog for, and I thought about how things could be a lot worse for him. At least he had a viable business. Not to mention a steady income. If he was seeking sympathy, I was the last person he should turn to.

Six

The next morning was warm and smoggy, and I spent the better part of the day sitting in my car outside of a beach house in Malibu. Looking through a pair of binoculars, I was feeling very much like a voyeur as well as feeling completely foolish. Young Violet, the dermatologist's wife, was doing little more than lounging around the sun deck with a girl friend, the two of them wearing skimpy bikinis and looking decidedly tantalizing. By two o'clock, they were both getting nicely tanned and I was becoming excruciatingly horny. Despite the sparkle of their lean, glistening bodies, I still would have preferred twenty minutes with Gail Pepper to half a day with either of them. Since it did not appear that any shenanigans would be enjoined today, I packed up the binoculars and headed back down to Bay City. Unlike the good doctor, I had doubts that Violet was engaging in any sexual liaisons, if indeed she ever had been at all.

The local Republican Party headquarters was situated along Wilshire Boulevard, on the fourteenth floor of a smoked glass office tower. The building was plush and quiet, as if there was either massive insulation or nobody was working on a Thursday morning. Even the air conditioning was silent. The subdued atmosphere continued as I turned the silver handle and walked into their office.

An attractive receptionist wearing a pleated white blouse that was nothing if not tasteful, turned from her laptop and said hello.

"Kind of quiet here," I remarked.

She sighed and nodded grimly. "The enthusiasm is quite low. May I help you?"

"I'd like to speak to Aaron Gregory."

"And your name?"

"Burnside. I'm a friend of Wayne's."

Her eyes widened as she picked up the phone and buzzed the intercom. A few minutes later I was ushered inside.

A grim faced man wearing a dark blue suit and maroon tie rose from his desk and shook hands with me. "Aaron Gregory. What can I do for you?"

"The name's Burnside. And thanks, but I'll pass on the coffee and Danish."

His mouth tightened. "Mr. Burnside, I am a busy man. Please spare me your sarcasm and tell me what you want."

"I'm a friend of Wayne's. And a private investigator. I'm looking into what happened the other night."

"On whose behalf?"

"For now let's just say on the behalf of Wayne's memory. Not to mention my own idle curiosity."

"Your own curiosity," he repeated. "Oh, hell. I'll give you a few minutes. I don't think the police are bound to do much."

"Tell me a little about Jim Callison," I started.

He fluttered his lips in a way that would have sprayed me with saliva if I were closer. He looked over at a portrait of Abraham Lincoln on the far wall. Honest Abe didn't look too happy about things either.

"Mayor Callison," he declared. "Where do I begin? The guy has had Bay City in his pocket for almost twelve damn years. Locked up. Everyone we ran against him got clobbered, he fit in so well here. This city may be the most left wing place in the whole country, and that includes Berkeley and Cambridge. We call this city the PRBC: the People's Republic of Bay City. And for years Callison was the classic liberal democrat, right out of the George McGovern wing. Put the guy in Mississippi and they'd tar and feather him but around these parts he was a God."

"Seems he lost his touch a bit. I heard Wayne was running even with him in the polls."

"You bet he was. And Wayne was going to knock him off. He was perfect. He had that Homeless Center so all the bleeding hearts in Bay City loved him. Plus he was a businessman so that sat well with the conservatives. And his timing couldn't have been better. Callison's contributors were revealed -- the biggest developers on the Westside were backing him. Kiss of death around here. Mention you're pro-growth and they'll clobber you. At the federal level, abortion is the acid test. Around here it's development."

"I take it Wayne didn't mention he was pro-growth."

"We convinced him not to. A compromise. The traffic's a problem for people and it's getting worse. They used to blame all the ex-New Yorkers. Now they blame the developers."

"But Wayne was a businessman. And a former real estate developer himself."

"Exactly. We positioned Wayne as a guy who was on the inside and saw the horror of it and backed out of the business. Sold all of his real estate interests."

"So you convince the liberals he's a liberal and the conservatives he's a conservative."

"You got it."

Just like I thought, politics was easy. Once you give up your values, everything else was a piece of cake.

"And Callison was in real danger of losing his job," I said.

"Right."

"And would have done anything to keep it."

"Right."

"Including murder?"

Gregory shrugged. "Wouldn't surprise me. Might be worth looking into...." he said, his voice trailing off.

A thought occurred to me. "Who's filling Wayne's vacancy on the ballot?"

"Lee Finley," he said. "Local Councilman. It'll be announced next week."

I frowned. "What are his odds? Must be a near impossible job to try and run someone new with only five weeks to the election."

"Isn't it though?" Gregory said wearily. "Finley's a good man but it's certainly not my idea of how to run a proper campaign."

*

The weekly workshop at Second Chance was to begin at six-thirty as scheduled. This week's topic was on how to interview for a job. It could have been postponed, but Jerry decided that Wayne would have wanted things to go on. No one was about to disagree.

Only three other volunteers showed up to assist the roughly fifteen homeless clients. The clients varied in age from twenty to fifty, and most were attentive and dressed cleanly. Second Chance worked in concert with two other homeless shelters in Bay City to provide training and job placement for those ready to re-enter the work force. That typically meant going through a screening interview with Jerry Winkler. If they came across reasonably well, they were placed in the program.

The other volunteers were Jerry, Amy Flanders, and a new volunteer named Matthew. Amy was one person I had yet to talk to; the car dealership she worked at kept telling me she was with a customer, and her voice mail kept saying leave a message and she'd get right back to me.

Jerry approached me before things got under way. "Light crowd here," he commented. "I guess some of our volunteers feel a little uneasy after what happened the other night."

I shrugged. "There's no need to be. This was no random act of violence. From what I can gather, there are plenty of people walking around with motives to shoot Wayne Fairborn."

"You don't think it was Crystal?"

"I'm not totally ruling it out, but I'd put my money on half a dozen others first."

Jerry nodded. "Have you considered Raff?"

"Sure," I said. "Still am in fact. Why?"

Jerry motioned upstairs with his thumb. "He came by earlier to pick up his paycheck. I caught him going through some things in Wayne's office. Said he was just dusting them off."

"Anything missing?"

"Not that I could tell," he said. "Then Raff said he had another job. Wasn't real specific and wouldn't tell me with who."

"When was he here?"

"About a half hour ago. I told him he was welcome to stay for the workshop but he insisted on having to leave. Strange thing, wouldn't you say?"

"Perhaps," I remarked and turned towards the podium. "But there's a lot of strange things going on here."

Jerry led the workshop, and gave a brief twenty minute synopsis on the do's and don'ts of interviewing for a job. He stressed the necessity of a clean appearance, an alert mind and most important, show a lot of interest in working there.

"You mean be enthusiastic?" one of the women asked.

He nodded. "Enthusiasm will get you a lot farther than brains." If they took nothing else from tonight's workshop, remembering that tidbit would help them inordinately.

Jerry then suggested we break up into groups of four or five and conduct some mock interviews. My group consisted of a gangly man whose name was Arthur Harris, a woman who said her name was Mary but preferred to be called Charmaine, a hefty guy named Lenny Mast who was built like a defensive tackle, and a little guy named Jimmy who observed attentively but said absolutely nothing.

I played interviewer and selected Mast as my first applicant. He told me in an outgoing demeanor that he was applying for a job as a chef.

"Okay Mr. Mast. What's your experience?"

"First of all, my friends call me Mustard."

"Mustard?" I asked quizzically, "why Mustard?"

"On account of I slap mustard on just about everything," he said, showing a toothy grin. "We was poor where I grew up. Back in southeast Arkansas. No matter how bad our meals were, putting a little hot mustard on things hid the taste just fine."

My palate blanched. "You might want to hold off telling that story until after you're hired," I suggested. "What about your experience?"

"I put four years in as a cook," he said proudly.

"Where?"

"San Quentin."

I closed my eyes. "Why don't you try saying 'a place up in the Bay area' or something like that? If they specifically ask if you were in prison then tell them the truth, but you do not have to volunteer it."

"Got it, man."

"Okay. What type of food did you cook at this place up north?"

"Soup, ravioli, chow mein. It was easy. Open up them giant cans and spill the whole mess into a big pot!"

I rubbed the bridge of my nose. "Try saying something like 'the place served a lot of different entrees. Like a coffee shop.' And you have experience cooking lots of different things. Basically what I'm trying to tell you is put your best foot forward. Make a good impression. Remember, there's nothing you can't learn once you get the job."

"Sure," the gangly man said cynically. "Then when you see somebody whose job you like better, you can set them up, get them fired and then take their job away. That's the way it is in the business world."

The bitterness exuded from him like smoke from a burning bush. "What's your story, Arthur?" I asked.

"I used to work for a bank. Big one, downtown. Spent ten years doing financial analysis. Had just bought a condo when the financial sector collapsed. So they brought in these new executives and decided to clean house. They didn't like my boss, so our department was the first to get riffed."

"Riffed?"

"R-I-F," he spelled it out. "Reduction in force. Sounds nicer than getting canned, don't it? Happened at the worst possible time too. I had just bought this condo. Invested every dime I had and when the job went, so did the condo. I missed four payments and the bank foreclosed. Lost everything. The bank stole my investment. Said they needed to recoup the loss they took when they sold it. Said the value had dropped a lot."

"Couldn't you have just gotten another job?" Charmaine asked.

"Try and find one," he sneered. "Oh, I could get a job that pays less than half what I was making before. Sure. Be a clerk somewhere. Or do data entry. Take a job that's beneath me. Uh-uh."

Charmaine glowered at him. "What you're turning your nose up at is probably more than I ever made," she countered. "What are you going to do? Wait until some high falutin' executive position come along again?"

"She's got a point, Arthur," I said. "You had it better than most people. Maybe you'll get there again. But it looks like you're going to have to prove yourself."

"I already proved myself," he said indignantly. "Why should I have to go pay my dues once more? Tell me why?"

I lowered my eyes for a moment. He was asking me why life was unfair and I had no answers. Like him, I had mostly questions.

"Arthur," I said softly. "If I could explain it, I'd have the key to the universe. One thing I can tell you though, is that the winners are the ones who hang in there. The ones who don't give up when they have a setback. Pick the job you want and become the person who does it."

He mulled that thought over and I hoped that it sunk in. I turned to Charmaine and asked what type of work she was looking for. She told me she was an actress.

"Have you worked in the industry yet?" I asked.

"Not yet," she said, her voice coated with a little anxiety. "I've been in a few productions back home, though. I had the lead role in *West Side Story*. I played Maria."

"Nice. Where's back home?"

"Iowa City."

"Seems like half the native Californians have roots in Iowa," I said. "That's where my great grandparents were from."

"From what I can tell, half the people here are from New York," she said.

"They're not natives," Arthur commented and added wryly, "and they never will be either."

Suddenly we heard the sound of a door slam and the pounding of shoes on linoleum. Three seconds later Jerry burst into the workshop room, his eyes wide and his breath coming in spurts.

"Burnside," he gasped. "I need you. You've got to come see this."

He turned and sprinted towards the door and I walked purposefully after him, my eyes darting up and down the street and my hand on the .38 just in case. I followed Jerry around the corner to an alley that ran parallel to the building. The alley was old and narrow with a few pathetic looking bushes and some milkweed growing haphazardly abound. A pair of ugly orange dumpsters stood amidst the urban foliage.

He pointed to the dumpsters. "I was putting some trash out," he exclaimed. "It's over there."

I walked up the alley and saw what appeared to be a very worn black boot sticking up next to the dumpster. Taking a closer gander, I saw the body it came with. The black frame glasses had slid down to the tip of his nose and his mouth was open. There was no pulse. No sign of life emanated from his body. Raff was dead.

Seven

Here we go again. Paramedics, local reporters, and of course the same law enforcement officials hovering on the scene, asking questions and munching sandwiches.

Detective Barney Sack delegated the task of interviewing me to a subordinate while he talked to Jerry Winkler. A broad shouldered hulk with closely cropped, white blond hair approached me. He had a notebook in one hand and a sandwich in the other. His name was Chuck Bausch and he looked as if he were more preoccupied with his dinner than in doing his job. Taking a large chomp out of a turkey and cheese on white bread, Bausch wiped a small glop of mayonnaise from the top of his chin. He motioned with his right hand for me to follow him into the hallway, his mouth too stuffed with food to be of any use.

"Let's get this done," Bausch said.

"Sure."

"You the one who found the stiff?"

I paused. "Raff."

"Huh?"

"His name was Raff," I said with growing impatience. I may not have been friends with the guy, but he deserved more respect than simply being called a stiff.

"Whatever."

I stared at him. "They run out of doughnuts, officer?"

Bausch looked at me hard and pointed his finger just like Sack had done. Maybe this was a Bay City cop thing. "A real smart ass. I heard about you and your antics. Get cute with me and you'll wake up looking at the dust bunnies underneath the prison bed."

"I'm quivering."

"You ought to be," he said, picking his teeth with a fingernail. "I want to know what happened here tonight, Burnside. Just the facts. None of your smart ass bullshit. You know the routine."

"Routine?"

"Yeah. The routine."

I feigned ignorance. "Time to round up the usual suspects?"

Bausch shook his head. "Again. You the one who found him?"

"Jerry Winkler found him, he's the director here. Somehow I don't think he did it. Unless you're going to bring in that reverse psychology logic Sack used last time. He tried to sell me on the idea Nina Lovejoy could have shot Fairborn."

"That little honey is still a suspect," he said, pointing a finger at me again.

I blinked. "You mean Crystal was released?"

"I mean as of this morning. Your sources are pretty lame there, bud. The wife is in the clear."

"Who do you have in custody now?"

"The case is still open. There may be a link with what happened here tonight. Not that I really give a damn who zapped that bum in the alley, but it may help us in the Fairborn case."

I felt my temperature rising. "Gee officer, do you really think the two murders are related? Just because they happened three days apart at the same location? And that the two dead guys were connected to Second Chance? Gosh, I wish I had your powers of deduction. I never would have considered such a possibility."

Bausch narrowed his eyes. "You're getting on my nerves, pal," he growled. "Just stick to answering the questions. Now, what could that guy Jerry have been doing in the alley? Giving some personal counseling?"

"Why don't you ask him?" I said.

"Because I got the badge," he said, the growl turning onto a snarl. "And I'm asking you. And I don't take no guff from no big mouthed private asshole. Somebody gets out of line with me, I'll rearrange their face."

"If you want to do some good in the world," I said, "why don't you start with your own?"

With that, Bausch threw down his clipboard and came at me, catching me with a left hook to my right ear. I winced and gathered up my reserves as quickly as possible. Fights like these begin and end quickly. Bausch knowingly grabbed my shirt with both hands and tried to jerk it over my head, which would have rendered me defenseless. As he tugged my shirt, I planted my left foot as solidly as I could and swung my right up into his crotch. Not as hard as I would have liked, but he nevertheless let out a yelp that told me my foot had done some damage.

The back of my shirt was pulled partway over my shoulders, but I managed to ball my left hand into a fist and let fly with a mean little punch. I hit him square in the right cheek and he grunted with pain. Actually, we both expressed some agony as I was quickly reminded that this was the wrist I strained trying to fend off Rusty Haas. Moving backwards, Bausch unexpectedly threw a right hand which caught me on the jaw. It didn't hurt so much as it served to give his crew a few more seconds to respond. Before I could do anything further, I was tackled by two burly plainclothes cops who slammed me to the floor and pinned my arms behind me. A pair of handcuffs were painfully applied, and at that point I would have given anything to be a one-armed man. My left wrist was searing with pain; if it wasn't broken, it was at least sorely sprained.

One of the cops hoisted me up by the elbow and I saw Bausch glaring at me with a murderous look. For a minute I thought he might actually hit someone in handcuffs.

"You just made a big mistake, pal," he roared at me. "Maybe a few days in the tank'll smarten you up."

Before I could come up with an answer, a deep voice boomed. "If there was a mistake, officer, it was made by you. I would strongly advise you to let this man go free."

I looked up and saw the looming figure of Virgil Hairston. He was pointing a large finger at the hunched over detective.

Barney Sack intervened quickly. "Who the hell do you think you are?

"I think I'm the one who's going to make that officer lose his job when half of Bay City reads about police brutality," he declared. "A cop who attacks a citizen for speaking his mind and then has him arrested for merely defending himself? You go through with putting this man in jail and I'll make you the sorriest bunch in town."

Sack looked around nervously and told Bausch to stop holding his crotch. "You with the Tribune?"

"You bet I'm with the Tribune. And if you don't take the cuffs off of that man immediately, your department will regret it for a long time."

Sack looked sheepish. "Okay," he finally managed. "Let him go."

The cop who lifted me up got out a key and slowly snapped the cuffs off, giving me a dirty look all the while. I rubbed my wrist delicately and looked at Hairston. He winked discreetly at me and smiled.

"The pen is mightier than the sword," he whispered.

My wrist was beginning to throb and felt as if it were a wet rag that had been wrung dry.

"Depends on whose wielding it," I pointed out.

*

A different officer took the rest of my statement, and not surprisingly it went a lot smoother. Hairston jotted down what he needed from the police P.R. rep and we soon adjourned to a little Mexican restaurant down the street. Hairston ordered *carnitas* and *frijoles*, and I had to scan the menu carefully before settling on two bottles of Dos Equis Amber.

"I keep hanging around with you and my cholesterol level may rise by osmosis," I said, eyeing the gooey plate with a mixture of envy and trepidation.

He rubbed his belly with his free hand. "I like to eat," he said, "and make no excuses."

"As do I. But getting handcuffs slapped on my wrists

tempers some of my appetite."

"You don't seem to have much of an appetite for good relations with the police either."

"We see things from different perspectives. They exist to maintain order. Justice isn't always properly served."

"That's where you come in?"

I shook my head. "Not very often. Only when it affects me personally."

"Why'd you leave the police force? You could accomplish a lot more on the inside."

I took a long swallow of beer. It was cold and strong and had a slightly bitter quality which suited my palate just fine.

"Well I left because they told me to leave. There was an incident, which I don't care to describe right now, that caused me to reconsider my values. And some of the top brass didn't appreciate a cop with an attitude. My new employer is far more lenient that way."

"Most people would like to work for themselves," he said. "I envy you."

"You forget the part about a steady paycheck, plush surroundings and health insurance. And the occasional physical altercation that comes with my line of work. Few things are as they seem."

"True enough."

"The police uncover anything on Raff?" I queried.

Hairston shook his head no. "I think they'll shitcan the investigation. One dead vagrant is nothing for them to sweat over, at least that was the impression they left me with."

"Have they found a link between Raff and Wayne?"

"No, other than the obvious. They didn't say how long it

would take to determine the murder weapon."

"Autopsy report could be ready quickly if they push it. Depends how busy the coroner is. Or how bad the police want to know."

"Think it'll be a .32 again?"

I nodded. "If I had any money, I'd lay odds it was. I don't believe in coincidences. Raff knew something and he had to be shut up."

"Sounds like someone's getting nervous."

"It happens when the stakes are high. Murder One carries a pretty steep penalty, particularly when it's a politician that gets smoked. Whoever did this is trying to cover their tracks."

Hairston chewed thoughtfully and shook his head. "This is the most excitement I've seen in Bay City since they passed rent control back in '79."

"That was probably less bloody."

"You might be surprised."

I finished my first beer and reached for the second bottle. In a ritzier establishment, champagne might have been in order. It wasn't every day you get to slug a cop and walk away from it.

"So what's the story on Crystal Fairborn?" I asked.

"Charges dropped," he said, through bites of his shredded pork. "That dried blood on Crystal's steering wheel turned out to be her own blood, not her husband's."

"Interesting," I remarked. "How'd it get there?"

"Said someone tried to run her off the road last weekend and she cut her hand on the dashboard during the collision. They also ran some tests on that business card you found sitting in Fairborn's lap. Crystal's fingerprints weren't on them.

Plus, Crystal said she wasn't even at Second Chance that night, and she even passed a polygraph test."

"And the eyewitness...?"

"Interestingly enough, she passed the polygraph as well. I guess those things aren't foolproof."

"True, but they're better than gut feeling. Amy's actually one person I haven't been able to talk with yet."

Hairston looked past me and offered a wry smile. "Now's your chance. She's been waiting there for a few minutes."

I turned around and saw Amy Flanders standing in the doorway. She was a fair skinned, buxom woman with short dark hair that fell across her forehead in bangs. Not unattractive, Amy had a tough look about her, like she had been around the block and then some. There were some men who liked that in a woman, but for me it was not very attractive. She wore a black cotton skirt with a gold striped blouse that revealed some cleavage. A gold necklace with a small heart dangled near her breasts. About a dozen thin gold bracelets hung from her wrist, looking as if they would surely fall off, but magically defied gravity. I waved her over.

"I was told I'd find you guys here," she said as she reached our table.

I rose and put out my hand. "I think we met the other night. I'm Burnside."

"Yes, I remember. And you're Mister..."

"Hairston," he answered, not bothering to rise.

"Right. It's nice to, well, I guess it's not *nice* to see you again under these circumstances. Can I, uh, join you?"

"By all means," I said. "I've been trying to get in touch the past few days."

"I know," she sighed, sitting down. "That's why I stopped by, I heard you might be here. I apologize for not getting back to you. This whole thing has upset me terribly. Wayne, as you might know, was a dear, dear friend. I've been in such terrible grief since this... thing happened. And now tonight. It's so horrible."

A waitress in a colorful off the shoulder dress came by and asked if we'd like anything else. Amy ordered a Margarita and Hairston asked for a Corona without the lime. I considered a third Dos Equis but finally passed. It was time to punch the clock again.

"How did you know Wayne?" I asked.

"I work for Liebross Motors," she told me. "I sold Wayne his Lincoln Navigator last year. We've remained friends."

"Did you know his wife very well?"

"Not exceptionally well. It was Wayne I knew. Of course, I knew of his wife, I mean everyone knows Crystal. I've been volunteering with the mayoral campaign and she's there a lot, obviously."

"So you're sure it was Crystal you saw leaving the Center the other night. No mistake?"

The waitress sat a Margarita down in front of her. The rim was lined with salt, and Amy took a lick of it before tipping the glass and enjoying a lengthy sip.

"I'm pretty sure. But I can't be a hundred percent positive. Not entirely, no." she said. "It was dark and all that. But it sure looked like her in the alley. And she was in a big hurry to get out of there."

"You know that the police cleared her today," I said.

Amy nearly choked on her drink. "They did?" she asked in

disbelief. "Who on earth do they think did it?"

"They're still unsure. Let me ask you something. The back exit at Second Chance leads to an alley around the corner. Why were you there?"

"Going to my car. Hey look, what do you want from me? I've already cooperated with the police."

I held up my hands. "Sorry. I've had a rough day. I didn't mean to offend you." If I had intended to, I thought to myself, I would have left little doubt.

"Okay," she pouted. "I'm still a bit brittle over this whole thing. I didn't mean to snap at you."

"Sure," I said as patiently as possible. "Did you see anyone else leave through the alley the other night?"

"I thought I saw Crystal. And I thought I also saw that homeless man who works at the Center. Oh yeah, and the girl who dresses like a street walker, Nina, I think her name was. She dates that guy who was there tonight."

"Mel?" I asked.

"Right. A real letch," she said, making a face. "I went out with him once. Thinks he's hot 'cause he owns a liquor store. What do I care if he owns a business? I've met men who could buy and sell him without blinking an eye. He and that slut Nina deserve each other."

"Let's think back to the alley the other night," I said slowly. "I want you to try and remember who came out first."

Amy answered without hesitation. "It was Nina, no question."

"And then?"

"Then another woman, it looked like it was Crystal. She was in a big hurry."

"How much time elapsed?"

"I dunno. A minute maybe."

"And then Raff came out?"

"Yeah," she said. "Maybe thirty seconds later. At least I think it was about thirty seconds."

"When did you hear the shots from the gun?"

She shook her head. "I didn't. There was a lot of conversation outside. I didn't hear about the shooting itself until the next day when the police called me."

"So if we assume that this young lady got it right," Hairston pondered, "there were three potential people who could have killed Wayne Fairborn. Actually two, if you exclude Raff."

"Not quite," I said. "There are those dumpsters sitting in that alley. They're about five feet high and plenty wide enough for someone to hide in until the coast is clear."

"So that expands the suspect list beyond Crystal and Nina," he sighed.

"Just a tad," I said.

"But why would they kill Raff?" Amy asked. "He didn't do anything."

"It may be about what he had seen or heard. And what he could say if he got the opportunity."

"So then Raff might well have been there... " Hairston started.

" ... and overheard Wayne being killed," I said, finishing the thought for him. "And perhaps he even knew what led up to it."

"So he had to be silenced."

"Yes," I said.

We paid the check and walked outside. Amy lit a cigarette and headed down a side street for her car. Hairston and I walked silently down the quiet boulevard, thinking our thoughts. As we passed a doorway, we happened to walk by a man lying in the street and sobbing. He appeared grimy and broken. An empty bottle of whiskey lay next to him. Maybe he was mourning something as well.

Eight

The funeral of Wayne Fairborn had a somber, reserved tone to it. There was no church ceremony and the graveside service, conducted by a Presbyterian minister, was brief and to the point. As the casket was lowered into the ground I felt a sense of loneliness more than grief. I thought of Wayne's goals and his sense of purpose in life. I thought of his good natured humor and his understanding that life was about people and not about money.

The feeling of sadness lingered beyond the funeral, and as I sat in my empty office with the sparse furnishings I felt the solitude even more. A picture of Gail Pepper sat on my desk, the bright, incandescent smile shining into my heart. Gail wasn't due back until Thanksgiving, a holiday that seemed like an eternity away. The moments Gail and I spent together were special and magical. The memories were like a salve which I could pull out and coat myself with when I was feeling low. Usually these memories made me feel warm. On this day however, they only served to remind me of what I did not have.

At the funeral I spoke briefly with Wayne's brother Peter, and he told me we could talk soon. That was fine by me; interviewing people was the last thing I wanted to do today. He expressed anger over the police department's lack of progress in finding Wayne's killer. Crystal came up and hugged me without saying a word, the expression on her face needing no further embellishment. I told her to call me if she needed anything. I recognized a few other people from Second Chance including Rusty and Sara, who tendered glares rather than hugs.

The next day I puttered around my apartment, thinking of things I needed to do but not really wanting to do them. An announcement came on the early news, which for L.A. began at four o'clock, that said Lee Finley had been chosen to replace Wayne Fairborn as the Republican candidate for Bay City Mayor. Life goes on, whether we want it to or not.

It had begun to grow dark outside, and I pulled myself from my malaise and drove over to Second Chance. Mourning was a very natural, necessary act, but I doubted the pain and anger inside of me would be fully released until Wayne's killer was apprehended. And the key to Wayne's murder seemed inexorably linked to Raff's. There weren't very many people who knew Raff, but I had to start somewhere.

I parked my Pathfinder at a parking meter along Pico Boulevard. Slipping my credit card into the meter, I cursed the idiot who decided that extra revenue could be garnered by extending meter hours until midnight. I learned of the new law the hard way when a ticket found its way to my windshield one evening. Fortunately, I was on a well paying case then. The only currency I was getting paid in these days were bumps and bruises.

Eddy Steele was busy emptying out a number of garbage pails on the second floor of the Center. He hummed a tune as he worked, a man seemingly at peace with himself and the world.

"Eddy," I called. "How are you?"

Placing the pail he was emptying on the ground, Eddy wiped his hand off and reached out to shake mine. "I'm good, doing good," he said.

Eddy Steele had been a clerk with the Post Office for about fifteen years, and had managed to support his affinity for both straight bourbon and betting on the horses. His deft ability at juggling addictions came tumbling down when he added crystal meth to the equation. His money disappeared quickly and he soon wound up in debt. His work, which had been spotty at best, became non-existent when he'd disappear for days at a time. He was evicted from his apartment two months ago and wound up at Second Chance shortly thereafter. We helped him get a room and a part-time job. The rest was up to him.

"Got a minute?" I asked.

"All the time in the world, my man. This what I call a light day's work. Seem like no one here today."

"Probably no one was. How's the job market?"

"It's tight, man. But I'm doing what you told me to. I'm going through the job openings every day. Got an interview set up for Monday with that company over near the L.A. airport. What's their name again, Direct Something I think."

"That's great, Eddy. Dress as nicely as you can. Smile a lot and be very agreeable. Give them a reason to hire you."

"Good ideas. They must have worked for you once."

"Once," I said, thinking nothing lasts forever. "You heard about Raff?"

Eddy nodded. "I heard. I hear everything that goes on. Too bad. Raff a weird little guy, but nobody should have to go like that. Real shame."

"I know. Eddy, what can you tell me about Raff? Anything at all would be helpful."

"You looking into Raff? Ain't that the cops' job?"

"It's not a high priority with them," I said.

Eddy emptied another wastebasket into the dumpster. "I know about that. Cops don't have much time for people like us. We just something they wish would go away."

I knew the feeling. "Had you met Raff before Second Chance?"

"Oh yeah. I seen him around the park. And over near City Hall now and again. They have that free lunch thing. Every day we can go and get sandwiches, a hot meal, things like that. Raff be there all the time. Me, I only go when I'm flat out busted. I still got some pride."

His face bore the lines of age and wear, but there was an expression in his eyes that said he wanted more from life. Maybe that desire led him down a treacherous path once, but I felt that spirit would eventually take him back. Dignity is a commodity that illuminates the trail.

"I know you do, Eddy. Tell me something. Who would know about Raff? Any friends, anyone he was close to?"

"Well, like I told you before, Raff, he's secretive. Kind of a lone wolf. There was one guy I knew of though. Fellow go by the name of Mustard. Raff and he got along 'cause Mustard was in the joint once. He called Mustard a political prisoner or some shit like that. Raff, he liked that. In fact, it was Raff that told Mustard about this Center here."

"Anyone else?"

"That about it," he said. "Nice funeral yesterday?"

I shrugged. "I don't know. Nice isn't a good adjective to

describe burying somebody."

"I tell you one thing," Eddy said, as he continued working. "It better than being cremated by the City and having your ashes tossed out with the trash. Just ask Raff."

"I wish I could," I said. There were quite a few things I would have liked to ask him. Walking into Wayne's office, I thumbed through the rolodex file and found the address of Lenny Mast. I pulled a silver pen from the pen stand and stopped in my tracks. There was something engraved in the base of the stand. Three initials. WJF.

*

Mustard's room was dark when I stopped by. Nearly everyone else I wanted to talk to had been at Wayne's funeral yesterday and I chose to give them a short break. After something this traumatic, people needed a little time to reflect on things before plunging back into their everyday lives. There was one group however, that was not likely to be mourning Wayne Fairborn's demise and I felt it was time to pay them a visit. I doubted they would cooperate if they knew who I was, so I decided to go undercover.

Their offices were located along Main Street in the Ocean Park section of Bay City. A few decades ago, this street was lined mostly with laundromats, pool halls, and seedy bars, but a regentrification effort on the part of the new Mayor helped alter the landscape. Trendy eateries, art galleries and fashionable boutiques had smoothed over the rough edges of the neighborhood, all but erasing its sleazy past. But like the indestructible cockroach, the sleaze simply moved elsewhere.

I walked into a stylish three story glass and steel building marked by a stunning atrium with a number of trees growing inside of it. There was a skylight on the ceiling that allowed some moonlight to shine on the circular marble stairway that led up to the second level. There was only a half moon out, so not that much light poured in. An insignia, T & R, was chiseled into the floor at the base of the stairwell.

The Callison campaign office was humming along briskly and there appeared to be a bevy of activity. A bank of telephones was partially filled and everyone seated there was engaged in spirited conversation.

"May I help you?" asked a slender girl wearing a green shirt and jeans.

"I'm looking to do some volunteer work on the campaign," I said. "Do you need any help?"

"Oh, sure," she said in a somewhat bored voice, and motioned me to follow her. She led me into a little office and had me fill out a card with my name, address, phone number, and special skills I could offer the campaign. I chose to keep the parts about being an outstanding pugilist and marksman to myself.

"Can you help out tonight on the phones?" the woman, whose name was Mariah, asked. "We're a bit shorthanded."

I agreed amiably and she led me over to an open phone and handed me a stack of questionnaires and a list of eligible voters in Bay City. They were taking a poll this evening.

"Just follow the instructions on the questionnaire exactly," she said.

For the next hour, I pried various pieces of information from people that went well beyond who they were going to vote for. Age, income, marital status, and education levels were freely given away by most who participated, although this was less than one-quarter of those I could even get to answer their phone. The other three-quarters respectfully declined, with the exception of one man who said he would notify the police if I bothered him again. I wondered what he thought they would do about it.

It was approaching nine o'clock and Mariah came by to let the interviewers know we were through for the evening. There was a little celebration going on down the hall and everyone was invited. About twenty people were sitting around a very plush conference room lined with soft leather chairs, the kind you can sink into and take a snooze. Eight bottles of white wine were open, and a large platter of cheese cubes and cut up vegetables were being attacked voraciously.

"What's the occasion?" I asked Mariah.

"We're way out in front. The Mayor has a twenty point lead in the poll you people just conducted."

"It's not hard to run against a dead man," I pointed out.

Mariah shrugged. "Lee Finley announced his candidacy yesterday and no one knows him. Been on the City Council for ages and he's got no name I.D."

"So you figure it's all sewn up."

"Well..." she started.

A tall grey haired man stepped into the conversation. "Nothing's sewn up if we quit campaigning," he said with a trace of annoyance in his voice. "Mariah, what's going on here?"

"Mariah says we've got the election in the bag," I offered innocently.

The man shook his head. "The hell we have," he said. "We're still up against some negatives, Mariah. I'm surprised at you. Fairborn's gone, but that doesn't mean our problems are gone with him."

"What do you mean?" I asked.

The man peered at me. "Who are you?"

"Burnside," I said, reaching out gregariously to shake his hand. "I've just started volunteering with the campaign. But from what I can gather, this election here is all over but the shouting."

"Kent Fisher," he said, pausing to size me up. "I'm Mayor Callison's campaign manager. I don't mean to be a downer, and certainly we appreciate and need your help. I just want to make sure we don't get overconfident here and assume we've got it in the bag."

"Like Dewey in '48," I offered.

"Who?"

I smiled. Not everyone had my appreciation for trivia. "Tom Dewey. The papers thought he beat Truman and ran with the headline that he won the Presidency. It was a little embarrassing."

"Sure," he smiled blankly, and shook my hand again. "Nice meeting you."

He walked away and Mariah's eyes shot daggers into me. "Thanks a bunch, whoever you are," she said sourly, and took a gulp of Chardonnay.

"Gee I'm sorry, I didn't mean to get you into a bunch of trouble," I lied. "But just what did he mean by the negatives may not be gone?"

"Oh," she said, "it's nothing."

"From the timbre of his voice, it sure sounded like something."

"Just politics as usual. I've been on the Mayor's staff for six years, and around politicians for ten more. They're all a little corrupt if you ask me. Sorry if I burst your bubble."

I took it in stride. "I've survived worse."

Nine

If you had to pick a town that best depicts the image of the laid back Southern California lifestyle, it could easily be Hermosa Beach. Lazy and sun drenched, it had enough surfers to bolster a casual atmosphere, but was far from the urban grit found in parts of Venice and Bay City. As I veered off Pacific Coast Highway and onto Twenty-First street, I did notice a couple of street people sorting through a garbage bin, looking for anything of value before the trash trucks came by later that morning. It seemed like the homeless were everywhere. The Great Recession sure hit a lot of people.

Peter Fairborn lived in a small bungalow about three blocks from the beach. The cottage had screens on all the windows and the exterior facade was painted a soft shade of pink. Some of the grey shingles on the roof were coming apart, exposing the tar paper underneath. In the driveway sat an old brown MG Midget convertible that had seen better days. As I walked up to the front door, I kicked a deflated volleyball out of my way. It bounced once and fell to a dead stop.

The door opened about sixty seconds after my knock, and a good looking man in his late twenties opened the door. He had what appeared to be a one week beard growth, although some guys managed to maintain that disheveled look indefinitely. He wore a pair of baggy, swim trunks that came down to his knees and had a myriad of colors splattered across them. A black tank top advertising a burger joint in Maui adorned his upper torso.

"Hey, dude. Glad you could make it."

"Hi Peter." I said, glancing at my watch which read seven-thirty. "Hope this isn't too early for you. I'm a morning person."

"No way," he said, inviting me into a living room one could barely describe as modest. "I'm up at the crack of light. Some righteous waves are coming in then, and I just roll out of bed and hit the surf. Breakfast comes later."

If Peter Fairborn was like some surfers I knew, breakfast consisted of Frosted Flakes eaten straight from the box. Or glazed doughnuts washed down with an Orange Crush. In the background I heard the low rumble of a Mister Coffee machine in action. At least he had some semblance of normalcy.

"Enjoy surfing?" I asked.

"It's my life, dude. It's what I love. Why not go for it?"

"If you can support yourself, why not indeed," I answered, sitting down in a musty old easy chair and making the mistake of trying to steady myself with my left hand. The wrist screamed out in pain. I winced and grabbed it.

"Arthritis?" he asked, more or less seriously.

"I'm not that old, son." If he made another crack like that I might put my one good hand to work.

"Just messing with you. So you and Wayne were buds. He always did like to pal around with a weird bunch. Writers, homeless, detectives. You name it."

I balled my right hand into a fist, then relaxed it. I tried to keep my temper at bay by breathing in through the nose and out through the mouth. "It's called judging people for who they are, kid. Not by what possessions they own."

"Yeah, well, with the money Dad left him, you'd have thought he'd be hanging around with a bunch of lawyers and investment bankers."

"He did some of that, too," I said. "Since you brought the subject up, is there any truth to what I've heard about you being cut out of your father's will?"

"Uh-huh. Dad wrote me out of it. Set up a little trust fund so I wouldn't starve, but basically he left nearly all of Grandpa's dough to Wayne."

"You must have been really ticked, huh?" I asked.

"Well yeah. I mean, of course. No one likes losing out on that kind of change. But what really got me is Dad said he'd reinstate me if I straightened myself out. He did it to motivate me. He sent me the copy of the will to show me he was serious. I got the message. Started working down at Dad's office and everything. Then Dad up and had a stroke six weeks later. He never got around to changing the will."

"Timing is everything," I sighed. "When did your father pass on?"

"Two years ago. I mean, Wayne was always his favorite 'cause he went into the business full tilt and all. I didn't begrudge him his share, I just wanted my piece of the pie."

"Did you ever tell Wayne this?"

"We didn't talk a lot, but yeah, he knew how I felt. I spoke with him a while back and he said he'd set me up with a surfboard shop. Just wait till I get this Homeless Center started, just wait until the election's over. Don't worry, I'll help you, but I'm too busy now," Peter said, his face becoming distracted. "I don't think Crystal wanted him to have anything to do with me. She's a real bitch."

I made a mental note and moved on. "Any animosity between the two of you? You and Wayne I mean?" I asked.

"Hey, no way dude," he said, defensively. "Don't even think about that angle. I didn't kill my own brother. That's crazy."

"Any idea who might have?"

Peter wrinkled his brow and concentrated. The feverish intensity of his thought process made me wonder if he'd hurt himself.

"I dunno. I thought the police were on the right trail when they picked up Crystal. I never trusted her. She was mad at Wayne for not helping out her sister Sara and that pig of a husband of hers, Rusty. Rusty the whale. You see him the other day at the funeral? The guy could barely fit into his suit! Man, what a lard ass!"

"How'd Wayne and Rusty get on?"

"Okay for a while. Wayne helped him and Sara buy that house in Redondo. Gave them the down payment. The blockheads screwed that up when Rusty got canned from his teaching job. Couldn't make the payments and Wayne wouldn't bail them out. Pissed Crystal off something fierce, Sara being her sister and all, but I don't blame Wayne for standing his ground. It's like Dad used to tell us. You want something, you got to earn it."

"But your father inherited his fortune, didn't he?"

"Sure, Grandpa bought the land, but Dad was the one who developed a lot of the property. Grandpa gave him a good start, but Dad made the most of it. Like I was going to. If only I didn't get a couple of bad breaks."

I felt a pang of sympathy, small, but it was still there. I tried to ignore it. "I have to admire you, Peter. You don't seem to have much bitterness in you towards your brother or your father. Losing out on a fortune would make most people pretty steamed."

"You can't look backwards," he said. "There's too much in life to be enjoyed. I surf every day, play volleyball on the sand, got a couple a steady babes that come by. I bartend a little for some coin 'cause the trust fund money only cashes out once a year. Got a lotta buddies. This is what it's all about. I wouldn't trade my life for Wayne's. We were just cut out for different things."

"That's a healthy attitude," I managed.

"Yeah," he said. "But, I was talking to Dad's attorney, you know, at the funeral. He said that Wayne had set up a will and named me in it. Most goes to Crystal, but I'll get a chunk. A cool five million bucks."

"And that suits you fine," I said, feeling my nose wrinkle at the thought of it.

"You got it, dude," he said, with a smile.

"What are you planning to put the money towards," I asked. "Franchise a bunch of surfboard shops?"

"Nah," he said, sitting back and cracking a broad smile, "That was more the family's idea for me. What's that old line? I think I'll spend oh, about ninety-five percent of it on wine, women and song. The rest of it I'll just blow."

I thought about the dwindling numbers in my own checkbook and sensed my pulse beginning to race. The deep breathing exercise didn't work so well the second time around, so I decided I'd better move on before Peter said anything else.

If my wrist was feeling better I might have backhanded him. Walking out, I noticed the deflated volleyball was now back in my path on the sidewalk. I measured my steps and kicked the soft rubber thing as hard as I could and watched it fly a good fifty feet before bouncing twice and stopping in the gutter. I hoped the ball was Peter's. Whatever pangs of sympathy I felt for him had disappeared into the cool coastal air.

*

I stopped for breakfast at a beachfront cafe and had a spinach omelet that was way too small and tomatoes that were shriveled and mushy. The slice of cantaloupe and small bunch of red flame grapes had grown lukewarm by the time my fork reached them. The waitress, a shapely beach bunny in short-shorts, never got around to refilling my coffee cup. Combine all that with the fifteen dollar check, and my breakfast turned out to be neither tasty nor cheap. Virgil Hairston's fat laden diet no longer seemed that terrible.

When I arrived back in my office, I listened to the two messages that were waiting for me on my voice mail. One was from Dr. Leary, the dermatologist, asking how the investigation into his wife was going. The second was from the property manager of my office, inquiring when I would care to provide him with a rent check. I was busy weighing how much urgency I should assign to either when a soft rapping could be heard on my door. I turned and saw Crystal Fairborn walk in with a large, thick boned man who was old enough to be her father. My finely honed detective skills told me that it probably was.

"I'm sorry for not calling first," she said in a subdued voice.

I waved my hand. "No apologies necessary," I said.

"Burnside, I'd like you to meet my father, Serge Markovich."

Markovich held out a huge paw. "It is pleasure to meet you," he said through what seemed to be a Russian accent. He gave me a strong handshake that was somewhere between decidedly firm and bone crushing.

"I take it you work with your hands," I commented.

"I am tile man," he said proudly. "I tile kitchens, bathrooms, anything around the house. You have house? You name, I tile."

"Fine," I answered dryly. "I'll keep you in mind for my summer home up in Arrowhead."

Crystal sat down daintily and looked straight at me. Her eyes bore the weight of fatigue, exacerbated by the absence of any makeup. On some women that meant they appeared sallow and ashen, but on Crystal, her innate beauty made her look vulnerable. Markovich remained standing and rested his big hands protectively on the back of Crystal's chair.

"I've heard the police cleared you," I said to her.

"For now," she shrugged. "They were very specific about that. I'm still a person of interest, whatever that means."

"I'm the last person who'll be an apologist for the police, but there was an eyewitness involved. When the cops have nothing else to go on, that means a lot."

"To them, maybe. Except I didn't do it. And I wasn't at the Center that night. I think the only way I'm ever going to get my name cleared is to find out who did this."

"That's absolutely right," I said.

She pursed her lips together. "I'd like to hire you to help me."

"I'm already on the job."

"Working for who?" she peered at me.

"Wayne."

A wave of anguish swept her face as the mere name of her husband dredged up some memories. The impact of a loved one's death lasts a long time, sometimes forever. From her expression, I could see Crystal was still trying to accept the fact that he was gone. Still hoping that some mystical beam would carry him back, telling her it was all a mistake. Figuring out who murdered him would never ease the sorrow, but might permit her to mourn in a way that wasn't so horrible. A way she could concentrate on her husband's life, his decency, his generosity and his kindness, without being preoccupied with defending herself from a homicide charge.

"Wayne was in a tough election," I said slowly, "and the other side was nervous. There may also be something that came to a head the other night."

Crystal tried to blink away some tears. "What do you mean?"

I tried to think of a way to put it to her that was delicate, yet got the message across. She was a grieving widow, and the last thing she needed to dwell on were people who were trying to destroy Wayne in a political race. But it was imperative that I ask these questions. This was a case that had blind alleys leading into blind alleys.

"Wayne knew a lot of women, didn't he?"

"Why of course, plenty of our friends were women."

"Ah, yes," I managed. "Did he know some better than others?"

"Hey wait a minute," Markovich snapped in a loud voice. "Show respect here. For the dead."

I stood up and looked him in the eye. "A man's been killed. For all I know he may have asked for it. But I'm grabbing at straws here. The deeper I get into this case, the greater the number of possibilities seem to be turning up. Every stone I uncover has three more stones hiding underneath it. Right now I figure there's at least half a dozen people who could have shot Wayne."

"Who?" he demanded in a heavy voice. "You give me names. I find out."

"You no find out," I said, in my best broken English. "I'm a licensed investigator and I know what I'm doing. You on the other hand are an angry father out for vengeance. You may hurt the wrong person or you may hurt yourself. If you want to help, you can sit down and let your daughter talk. I'm doing the best I can to unravel this, which I might add is *pro bono*, and one thing I don't need is some big moose stomping around, muddying up the waters."

I kept looking him in the eye, wondering if he'd answer with his mouth or fists. His chest rose and fell rapidly but his mouth stayed zipped and his hands remained at his side. Good thing for both of us. I didn't think my wrist could take a lot more.

"I was going to tell you the other day," Crystal said softly, her voice having a vacuous quality to it. "You asked about a woman named Amy Flanders."

"Go on."

She bit her lip and looked beyond me out the window. I doubted she saw anything more than a few old ladies waiting at the bus stop. The wheels inside of her head seemed to be spinning, and whatever images they produced did not make her happy. A few new tears formed in her eyes.

"It happened just a couple of weeks ago," she said with a sniffle. "It was a package someone sent to Wayne but I opened it. No name, no return address. Just a package sent with a DVD inside. I watched it for a minute and at first I thought it was porn. Somebody's idea of a joke. Then the camera zoomed in for a close-up and it was Wayne. It was Wayne!"

She tried to choke back the tears but they were pouring out by now. She brushed a few away and continued.

"I was so furious," she said. "Wayne and I have been married for years. We met in college and it was a storybook romance."

"Rich boy meets poor girl," I remarked.

"Yes. I was at SC on a scholarship, Wayne was getting an MBA. He was so handsome and smooth, he could have gotten any girl he wanted. I used to pinch myself because it seemed like such a dream. And our marriage had been wonderful. I couldn't understand what had happened."

"Did you confront Wayne with the tape?"

"Oh you bet I did," she said through wide, glistening eyes. "He admitted the affair, said it was the first time, said the woman seduced him. And he said it would never happen again."

"And you believed him."

"He said he made a mistake. I was angry, I was bitter. I tried to look at what I could have done to have prevented it from happening. I blamed him, I blamed myself. I was trying to forgive him. To let him have a second chance."

"And the woman he was with was Amy?" I asked.

Crystal nodded.

"Was she the one who mailed the DVD?"

"I don't know who mailed it. After I confronted Wayne, we had it out. But from that point on we never discussed it again. I didn't bring it up and neither did he."

I cringed as I watched the shiny tears roll down Crystal's smooth cheeks. "I'm sorry to have to put you through all this," I said. "I know it's difficult, but this is part of my job. I like to think I'm good at it."

"You are," she said. "And you also mentioned you were working *pro bono*. If Wayne hired you, why are you doing it for free?"

"Somebody killed him before we could agree on a price."

She frowned. "What do you normally charge?"

"Seven hundred a day," I said.

She took out her checkbook and wrote me out a two week retainer. The stubborn streak in me wanted to tell her this was on the house. That this investigation was something I was doing out of loyalty to Wayne and compassion for his memory. My pragmatic side told me I might soon be evicted. Two forces, diametrically opposed.

"I appreciate the fact that you've involved yourself already," she said, pressing the check into my hand. "I'm fighting for my life here. Nobody else could want to help me more than you. I heard that message from your landlord when we were walking in. I know you need the money. And right now I need you."

With that she stood up and walked out the door, her father following in tow. I took a deep breath and mulled things over. One could easily scratch Crystal off the list of suspects, but in so doing it would be just as easy to pencil in Markovich.

The phone rang at that point and I grabbed it before it could go to voice mail. I'd have to either reduce the volume or else start listening to these messages with my door shut.

"Hey Burnside," the voice came across the line. "This is Jerry. I'm okay, but some new evidence turned up last night at the Center. It's a whopper, too."

"What's that?"

"The gun," he said. "A .32 caliber pistol. Somebody planted it in my desk."

Ten

The police had come by the night before and grilled Jerry for the better part of the evening. Apparently they seemed satisfied with what he said and little would be accomplished by detaining him. They fingerprinted Jerry and planned to have Ballistics run some tests on the gun. Sounding more than a little concerned over the phone, he asked if I could find out anything. I told Jerry I'd do what I could and would try to swing by Second Chance in the morning. Putting the phone down, I wondered what in hell could happen next.

There were two people I needed to speak with and both were temporarily *incommunicado*. Mustard's room was still dark and Barney Sack had yet to arrive at work. Sack's shift went from four until midnight, so I amused myself for a while down on the Bay City Pier. Having a few extra dollars in my pocket, I played some video games, got out some aggressions in the bumper cars, and flung two out of three footballs through a small black tire. I noticed half the patrons at the Pier were street people, and the once pleasant, carnival atmosphere had turned unsavory. I succumbed to a few requests for money, figuring if I was spending money this frivolously I should at least be a little generous with some of it. When I saw one of my recipients swagger by later with a can of Budweiser, the warm, benevolent feelings vanished.

At four o'clock I went over to police department headquarters and found the pudgy detective sitting in his office, loading bullets into his service revolver. He had on a beige shirt open at the collar, with a green and yellow striped tie pulled down past the second button. Even at the shift's commencement, Detective Sack had the rumpled look of one who had already survived a demanding day.

"Hope my name isn't on one of those bullets, detective."

Sack glanced up and a faint look of disgust crossed his face. On Sack it looked as normal and proper as palm trees swaying on a tropical beach.

"Ah Christ, look what the smog blew in," he muttered.

"Smog doesn't blow, detective. It just sits there looking ugly."

"I do hope," he said, "you didn't mean anything personal in that crack. For your sake."

I raised my hands. "Touchy, touchy," I said. "The last thing I want to do is insult a man loading his weapon."

"Uh-huh," Sack said, snapping the pistol together and jamming it into his holster. "So what's up? Any more dead bodies turn up at that house of bleeding hearts?"

I sauntered into his office. "My, we are cynical, aren't we? A few people trying to do some good in the world and all you can do is criticize?"

"Do some good," he chuckled cynically without bearing a smile. "Two murders. That's doing a lot of good. Why don't you expand and open things up to the whole Southland? I don't know what you've done for the homeless problem, but you're making real progress helping to limit the population growth in Bay City."

I sucked in some air. There were times to be insolent and times to put your wit in check. The last time I enraged one of Bay City's finest I ended up wearing a set of bracelets for a brief time. Discretion is sometimes warranted.

"As much as the idea intrigues me, I really didn't stop by for a discussion of contemporary sociological issues."

"What do you want then?"

"Answers to a few questions, perhaps?"

"Ah, Christ," he sighed, and looked at the clock. "Aw right, the watch doesn't begin for five more minutes. Get it over with."

"You're all heart, Sack. Jerry Winkler told me that Ballistics is running tests on the pistol. And I take it the killer is still at large."

"Last I looked," he snarled. "Yeah, the murder weapon turned up with Winkler, but I'm sure it was wiped clean. I doubt we'll get any prints off it. But it turns out the gun was registered to Fairborn himself. We'll get the Ballistics report in soon, but it's pretty obvious this is the gun that did it."

"Same person did them both, then."

"You're a genius, Burnside."

"What else can you give me?"

Sack sneered at me. "A boot in the pants if you keep getting in our way. You know, if it wasn't for that fat assed reporter you'd still be cooling your heels in the tank. This is police business and if you keep sticking your nose in it, I'll see to it it's clipped off for good."

I sighed. "Look, I have an obligation here. To the client I'm working for now, but also to the two guys who got killed. Fairborn's legacy will live on with Second Chance. But Raff's legacy died when he did. Somebody killed them. Somebody has to pay."

"And I got an obligation to the people that I work for," Sack said.

"Meaning?"

"Meaning I've been told this is low priority."

"Investigating Raff?" I asked.

"Investigating both of them."

"Since when are two murders low priority? Are you getting pressure from the Mayor's office?"

"You figure it out."

I took a deep breath. It was possible Callison simply wanted this mess swept under the rug and forgotten by the time election day rolled around in early November. It was also possible he had a more personal reason for wanting it to disappear.

"You want this case to go away too, Sack?"

"I want what the people who pay my salary want."

"Isn't that the good people of Bay City?"

It was Sack's turn to sigh. Maybe he did have some soul buried down there after all. "Look Burnside, I've been on the job here for almost twenty years. I stayed around by being a good soldier. By learning to follow orders. Yeah, I'd like to clear up this mess. Any way you slice it, unsolved murders don't look good for either a police force or a community. But I don't want some hot shot doing my job for me. And then having people ask why the police couldn't crack the case."

I shook my head. "I'm not looking for any headlines out of this," I said. "I don't want any glory. And I don't want to do your job for you. But a guy I know is dead and now somebody who probably had nothing to do with this, except maybe seeing something he shouldn't have, is dead as well. I respect your situation. I know your hands are tied."

"Damn straight."

Our eyes met for a moment. Sack was a survivor, the kind of cop I was afraid I'd become one day. Play by the rules, don't go against the tide, avoid making waves. When my moment of truth faced me, I knew I could never live by that arrangement. I learned I was not someone who would compromise, not somebody who could walk away from a situation I felt was patently unjust. There would always be guys like Sack. I just couldn't be one of them.

"I'll tell you what," I said. "As you probably can guess, this is not a case I can drop."

"So I'm seeing."

"But I'm not looking to embarrass anyone. Not even that goon that took a swing at me the other night. If I come up with anything, the glory's all yours."

"A big if."

I was about to make a smart comment, when I reminded myself again about discretion. I also recognized there was a fair chance that Barney Sack might be right.

*

It was nearly five o'clock and in Southern California that meant traffic was about to hit critical mass. If you had to travel by freeway it meant you were going to be in your car for a while. If you didn't have to get on the freeway, you steered clear at all costs.

I climbed into my Pathfinder and sat for a few minutes, letting the engine idle in neutral. I rolled the case around in my mind and tried to make sense of what I had. Raff, Nina and Crystal were identified as leaving through the back door of Second Chance after Wayne was killed. Crystal denied even being there and the more things I uncovered about the eyewitness Amy, the more I leaned towards Crystal's version.

I considered more players. Amy herself was far from being an impartial observer, and the fact that she had a liaison with Wayne made her a suspect. Peter Fairborn would now receive a financial windfall as a result of his brother's death. Crystal's father was taking a keen interest in the case. Her brother-in-law Rusty resented Wayne for not helping him more. Mel Fenster couldn't have been pleased with Wayne's involvement with Nina. Wayne might have had other women too. And I hadn't even scratched the surface of Mayor Callison's potential motives. With all that, my hopes for a quick solution to this case were not likely to be realized.

I flipped through my notebook and came across Nina Lovejoy's work address. Her magazine was headquartered in a slick black glass building along Wilshire Boulevard just west of the San Diego freeway. Nina's own office was located on the eighteenth floor, and as I pushed open a door which read *Tomorrow's Woman* in big brass lettering, my olfactory passages picked up the scent of jasmine and lilacs. I strolled onto the thick pile carpet that made my feet feel as if they were walking on marshmallows. Indirect lighting against the mauve walls lined the perimeter of the vestibule. At a chrome lined counter, a young girl wearing a lavender dress and a pink scarf hanging from her neck looked up. Her face had enough cosmetics layered on to hide not only her acne, but whatever distinguishing features may have formed. I told her I'd like to see Nina Lovejoy.

"Do you have an appointment?" she asked.

I removed my business card and handed it to her. "It's about an investigation I'm conducting. I think she'll see me."

The girl took the card and her brown, doe eyes grew wide. "Oh my. One moment please."

She left the vestibule and walked inside. Emerging a minute later she asked me to follow her. The inside of the office was decorated in much the same tone as the reception area, the hallways sporting plenty of soft pinks and purples, along with the occasional vase of flowers sprouting up from a table.

Nina's office was small enough to contain just a desk and a couple of chairs but the view from her window was stunning. With the Bay City mountains as a backdrop, she had a panoramic view of the Los Angeles basin, smog levels permitting. Today was not a good one from a visibility standpoint, as even nearby Westwood Village was little more than hazy shades of grey.

"Well this is a surprise," Nina said, waving a hand towards one of the chairs. I closed the door and sat down. Nina Lovejoy looked as lovely as ever, her pretty face displaying a marvelous peaches and cream complexion. Her long blonde hair was tied back into a golden pony tail that was shiny and lascivious.

"I'd say I was just in the neighborhood but you might have trouble swallowing that."

She smiled playfully. "I don't think I'd have trouble swallowing anything from you."

Whoa. I wasn't sure if I wished I was fifteen years younger or she were fifteen years older. "I'll remember that for future reference."

"A lot of men get intimidated when they meet a woman who knows what she wants and has no problem being up front about it."

"That's because we, as men, have been trained since kindergarten to be the aggressors. We're now being told to let go of our pre-conceived notions."

Nina nodded enthusiastically. "That's one of the things I love about my job. This magazine is exploring how people will live in the future."

I lifted up the October issue of *Tomorrow's Woman* and didn't go any farther than the slinky girl on the cover. A cursory look at the main stories indicated how women could find the hot man of their dreams, leap up the corporate ladder, and rule their world by the time they were thirty. I wondered if there would be anything left to achieve by the time they turned forty.

"Hopefully the future will be a bit less violent," I said, watching the exhilaration melt from her face.

"Yes," she managed. "That would be nice. I guess you're still looking into Wayne's tragedy."

"Don't tell me you've forgotten," I peered at her.

"Of course not," she scoffed. "But I've chosen not to think about it. It's a very painful experience and the mere thought of it upsets me. I believe positive thoughts beget positive energy. That's another thing the magazine teaches our readers."

"Uh-huh. Well I'd appreciate it if you would be so kind as to indulge me in a little pain for a few minutes."

Her features stiffened. "I suppose. If we must."

"We must," I said in as tender a voice as I could muster. Burnside, the sensitive soul. Lord help us all.

"First thing," I said, "is do you know anything at all about why Raff was killed the other night."

"Raff?" she asked with a tilt of her head.

"He was one of the homeless men going through the program at Second Chance. He was hired on recently as a janitor and somebody shot him outside the Center. Short guy, black framed glasses...?"

Nina nodded. "I remember. The Marxist."

"Marxist," I mused. "That doesn't surprise me."

"Why's that?"

"He was studying political science at UCLA," I said. "A lot of people in that field start out as Marxists. It's one of the fundamental bases for political thought."

"For a detective, you seem to know an awful lot of things."

Talk about a left-handed compliment. "Let's just say I have a talent for taking bits of trivia and piecing them together so they mean something."

"Did you go to college, Burnside?"

"Sure. Four years at USC. Earned a degree in Social Science with a minor in college football. I started out admiring Sigmund Freud and B.F. Skinner but ultimately I became more impressed with Ronnie Lott and Troy Polamalu."

"Are they psychologists?" she frowned.

"Safeties. Toughest pass defenders the NFL's ever seen. They both played at USC."

"Oh, yes. You men are into those sorts of things, aren't you."

"Indeed," I said. "But back to Raff. Any idea why someone would want him dead?"

She shook her head. "No more than I would understand about Wayne. This whole subject is not only disturbing, it's baffling."

"You're telling me. You know Nina, we never had a chance to talk about you and Wayne. When I told you about Wayne's death the other night, you were too upset to focus on much of anything. Can we do that now?"

She nodded cautiously. "What exactly do you need to know?"

"Were you and Wayne having an affair?"

The peaches and cream cheeks turned crimson in a hurry. Her mouth opened slightly, an automatic response perhaps, and she blinked a few times before regaining her composure. For a moment I thought I saw her actually gulp. Maybe not. Not Tomorrow's Woman.

"That's really not a concern of anybody's."

"Actually it is. It's a concern of mine because it may have had something to do with Wayne being killed. I'm not saying it did, mind you. There are plenty of avenues to go down in this case. But Wayne's infidelity has already been documented. I just need to know the extent of it."

Nina put a fingertip to the corner of her eye but I couldn't be sure if she was brushing away a tear or a piece of dust. Either way, she didn't look like a happy camper.

"What do you mean Wayne's infidelity has been documented?"

"I mean somebody recorded him copulating with another woman. Not his wife I should add."

"Oh my," she exclaimed. "Was it recent?"

That one remark spoke volumes. She looked shocked and her mouth was slightly open. I wondered if she was planning to schedule an STD test soon.

"We can't tell from the DVD," I said.

"Who was the woman?"

"Relax, it wasn't you."

Nina's mouth opened wide for a second and then closed quickly. It appeared she had found out her wayward lover had cheated on her.

"We only did it twice," she said slowly. "But both times were the most wonderful experiences. The things we shared, the things we felt. It was just so special. He told me he didn't love his wife anymore, and I was the first woman he had been with in a long time."

I suppose everything is relative. For Wayne, a long time might have been a week or two. Nina took a handkerchief from her purse and blew her nose daintily.

"I take it this was a more meaningful tryst than your relationship with Mel," I said, watching her eyes carefully.

"Mel? Mel and I don't have a relationship. Oh, he and I have gone out several times, but he's more of a friend than anything else. I think he'd like it to be more than that, but believe me there's no passion. Not like with Wayne. Wayne was like a... a magnet. I was hopelessly drawn to him. I couldn't say no to Wayne."

"So you have nothing going on with Mel then."

"No. Of course not."

"He seems to think otherwise," I said. "In fact he seems to think you two are deeply involved."

She gave me an odd look. "No," she said. "A relationship with Mel is simply not going to happen."

I thanked Nina for her time and stood up to leave. She looked at me, a little crestfallen at what she had just learned. No positive energy was exuding from her when I left her office. A little reflection on things perhaps, and maybe that wasn't so bad. Mulling things over could bring about a new direction in a person's life. It might not yield positive energy immediately, but all good things need time to percolate. I didn't bother to share that with her though. She had swallowed enough for one afternoon.

Eleven

Feeling rather exhausted, I decided to give myself a night off and stretched out on the couch for an ambitious evening of Monday Night Football. When the Jets took a 7-0 lead against the Steelers, I closed my eyes during the commercial break. When I reopened them, the next thing I saw was an old Eddie Murphy movie flashing across the screen. The clock read 1:22. I flicked off the TV and stumbled into the bedroom, vaguely wondering who won the game.

When you fall asleep too early in the evening, there is a distinct tendency to rise too early in the morning. At four-thirty my body told me I had slept enough. I got up and fixed a pot of coffee, and sipped on it while I skimmed various news websites. I was feeling edgy and needed to do something, but doubted anybody would appreciate a pre-dawn visit from a private investigator. I had enough trouble pleasing people during the light of day. Since my gym wasn't open yet, I donned a pair of shorts and journeyed out for an early morning jog.

I ran over to Palisades Park, which is a narrow strip of grass that overlooks the Pacific. Spanning just over a mile, it also served as a campground for the homeless. It had been a while since I had gone running this early, and I was awestruck at the number of homeless campers. With bodies strewn about the park, I couldn't help wondering if this was what Normandy looked like on the dawn of the invasion. I tried to find a straight path to run in, but all lanes had obstacles in them. A jogger about fifty yards ahead of me solved the problem by treating the course like it was the high hurdles.

The sun was fighting through the smog, and the yellow haze of the morning did little to perk up my spirits. After a shower, I went to the office and checked voice mail. Another message from the dermatologist. What was happening? Had I learned anything about Violet's activities? Why hadn't I called? I sighed and decided to pay him a visit. I was also starting to wonder why his wife wasn't having an affair.

The doctor's office was on the tenth floor of the Neudorf Medical Arts Building along Bay City Boulevard. As I walked into the waiting room, I was greeted by a receptionist who could easily have been a contestant in the Miss California pageant. Her wavy blonde locks swirled past her shoulders and the green eyes were as enticing as a kitten's. While she was wearing a professional looking white lab coat, the only thing under it was a black halter top and a pair of form fitting black jeans. She hadn't bothered to button the smock and I was not about to voice a complaint.

"Good morning," she smiled. "Do you have an appointment to see Dr. Leary?"

"No, actually I don't."

"How may I help you then?" she asked.

I handed her my card. She picked up the phone and punched in a number, speaking quietly into the receiver. Hanging up, she rose and asked me to follow her. The white coat flowed behind her and she led me down the hallway into the doctor's business office.

The doctor had on a white lab coat of his own, but he chose a light blue oxford shirt underneath, with the top three buttons open. A plethora of grey chest hair spilled into view. When he had initially come to solicit my services, he had the candor to at least wear a tie. Another pretty young woman, slender and dressed in a red tank top and jeans, sat across from his desk. For a moment I thought I had wandered onto a set of The Bachelor.

"The famous Mr. Burnside," crowed the doctor. "Ladies, let me introduce you to a real life detective."

The girls turned and looked impressed. "Are you like Magnum, P.I.?" asked the young thing in the red tank top. "My mom used to love that show."

"Precisely. Except I'm not as hairy and I punch harder."

"Ladies, would you excuse us," Dr. Leary said. "We have some private business to discuss. The detective probably wants my expert opinion on a medical matter. Brandy, why don't you show Lorelei how to work the coffee machine."

They left the room and as I closed the door, the dermatologist's effusive smile disappeared.

"Whaddya got for me?"

I raised my eyebrows. "Brandy?"

Leary shrugged. "The blonde. Lorelei's just starting today. Student nurse, wants some experience as she works her way through school."

"Making coffee's great RN training."

"There are worse internships. Anyway, when you make the kind of money I do, you can have some nice stuff walking around. I didn't bust my ass all these years to have a bunch of cows in here."

"Is that what you told your first wife?"

Leary glowered at me. "Now don't you crack wise. I hired you to find out about Violet. How come I haven't heard from you?"

"Because she hasn't done anything," I said evenly. "I talked to her girlfriends, her hairdresser, even the guy who clips the hedges outside your house. What I've come up with is *nada*."

"Keep snooping. She's up to something."

I sighed. "Just what makes you think that?"

"I hear things," he said. "Besides, I want to make sure, if for no other reason than my own piece of mind. One of my buddies at the club has a younger wife and one day he caught her with some tennis pro."

The good doctor's face was turning scarlet as he probably thought of his own lady love diddling someone closer to her own age.

"How long have you been married, doctor?"

"Two years to Violet."

"And to your first wife?"

"Thirty years. I figure I got about twenty more good years left in me, and I might as well enjoy them more."

Things probably would be fine for a few years, I admitted. But when the body parts start malfunctioning and those romps in the afternoon become fewer and more far between, a young women will probably start looking elsewhere. Someone you've been with for thirty years will doubtlessly be more compassionate. Especially when their own skin is sagging and they have as many maladies as you. His first wife was probably attractive once. It's a shame that nature never leaves well enough alone.

I tried a new tact. "So you think Violet's getting it elsewhere."

"Yeah, that's what I think."

"How about you. Have you been getting it elsewhere, too?"

"That's not your business, Burnside," he sneered. "Stick to looking through peep holes. I paid you three days retainer and you haven't come up with anything yet."

"And I've put a week into it already. If you have any doubts, I'll show you the log I've kept on her. It'll be included anyway in your final report."

Leary waved the idea away and opened his checkbook. " I owe you what, seven hundred a day?"

"Plus expenses." I hesitated before continuing. "But are you sure you want to keep doing this?"

He scribbled out a check for another three days pay. "You let me decide how to spend my money. This'll keep you going. Look, Violet sees a personal physique trainer every week. He's the one I really suspect. I'll get you the details. If nothing happens, I'll end the investigation."

I pocketed the check and winced as I stood up. The pain in my wrist was almost as strong as the one grinding my pride. I needed to stop using the arms of chairs as leverage. I also needed better clients, health insurance and a summer home up the coast.

"What's the matter?" he asked.

I held up my hand. "Banged up my wrist. I don't suppose you'd be able to help."

Leary shook his head. "I'm a dermatologist. Doctor of the skin," he said reaching into a file. He handed me a business card of an orthopedic surgeon named Don Gieselman. "He's a golf buddy of mine. Tell him I sent you. He'll give you a good rate."

I fingered the card and headed for the lobby. As I passed the pretty blonde receptionist, she motioned to me.

"Are you investigating Dr. Leary?"

"No. Why do you ask?"

She looked around carefully before replying. "He's a real creep. Can't keep his hands off the girls. Nobody lasts around this place."

"How come you're still here?"

She bit her lip. "I need this job badly. Money's tight. But I don't know how much more of that damn doctor's groping I can take."

I nodded. "Let me think about what I can do. There's always options. And I don't think you have to worry too much."

"Why not?"

"The world never lets a beautiful woman starve."

Getting one last smile from Brandy, I tossed the orthopedic surgeon's card in the trash and walked towards the elevator.

*

There's something very nostalgic about the candy section of a pharmacy. They often have hard-to-find treats that most convenience stores don't stock. The pharmacies' clientele is often older and more likely to be interested in items beyond M&Ms and Milky Way bars. The pharmacy on the ground floor of the Neudorf building evoked memories of childhood that brought a big smile to my face. Everything from Sky Bars to

Cup o' Gold to boxes of Good n' Fruity were sitting in the pharmacist's bin. I settled on a roll of Regal Crown Cherry Sours and happily let one of the lozenges dissolve on my tongue as I drove along the now sunny streets of Bay City.

For years now, anyone in need of a free meal could get one near City Hall. The program was sponsored by a wealthy donor who was concerned about people going hungry in the streets. With some logistical help from the city in the form of manpower and the use of municipal land, a free lunch was served daily. While some considered the program a booming success, others felt it attracted too many homeless people to Bay City where they stayed on, in a perpetual state of limbo.

When I first met Wayne, he told me how he had become tired of homeless people asking him for money on the street. As an experiment, he offered to take a panhandler to a local coffee shop and buy him a free meal. Over a hamburger, he learned that the people were usually not hungry, as they knew which missions and soup kitchens to visit for food. An extra meal was not to be scoffed at, they said, but they preferred cash so they could buy some personal items. For some people this could mean toothpaste and shaving cream, for others it could be a bottle of cheap wine.

A line had formed around a table where a group of volunteers and City Hall administrators were spooning out bowls of stew into plastic bowls. I looked around for the elusive Mustard, but he was nowhere to be seen. Walking down the line of those waiting for food, I asked each one if they had heard of him. Finally, a rangy looking man who could have passed for a corporate executive if he had a haircut and a new set of clothes said he thought he knew him.

"Big fat guy?" he asked.

"Yes." I concurred.

"Spent time in the can?"

"Right."

"Thinks he's a food expert?"

"Sounds like you know him."

"Yeah, sure. He hangs around the Promenade a lot. Says he gets a kick out of sitting next to those she-she restaurants and smelling what they're cooking. Cripes, but you meet all kinds around this place. Me, I'd rather eat the stuff, you know?"

"Sure."

"Anyways, you can usually find him hanging around the Third Street Promenade. Just look for a fat guy with his nose in the air."

"Got it," I said, and then tried a long shot. "Did you know a fellow named Raff?"

The would-be executive cackled. "His first name Riff?"

The world has no shortage of comedians. Thanking the man for his time, I handed him two dollars. Wayne wouldn't have approved, but everyone has their own value system. I looked at it as paying for information. Besides, I'd tipped far more in restaurants for service one could barely call acceptable.

I was about to leave when I noticed one of the workers on the soup line being replaced with a familiar face. I walked over to her and said hello.

"Oh, not you again," Mariah muttered. "Haven't you gotten me into enough trouble?"

"Trouble?" I asked.

Mariah said nothing and spooned a ladle of stew into a bowl, tossing a piece of bread on top. She repeated this for a few minutes without saying a word, and I repeated my question.

"Look, I don't know who you are," she said in a low voice so no one else could hear, "but I don't think I can help you. In fact, I think I have enough problems as it is. Thanks in part to you."

"You said that before," I mentioned. "Maybe I can help you."

"I doubt it. Unless you can help me get another job."

"You're not on the campaign anymore?"

She nodded and kept ladling. "I've been reassigned. To some low level admin post that I had five years ago. And all because Kent Fisher overheard our conversation and thinks I have a negative attitude. You didn't exactly help me out the other night. That comment you made to Fisher sent him into a tailspin."

I shrugged. "Sorry. If you're interested in a little revenge, I might be able to provide you with that."

"What are you, a paid hit man?" she scoffed.

I opened my jacket slightly to reveal the hardware under my armpit. "Only if the price is right."

She gaped at me. I suggested we go somewhere private and she called over one of her associates, a thin young man wearing a black sweater to replace her on the lunch line. We walked down the street together, moving slowly, as we had no particular destination.

"Tell me you're a cop."

"Private investigator."

She took a deep breath. "You weren't really volunteering the other night to help Callison."

"No. I'm actually investigating the murder of Wayne Fairborn."

Mariah gave a low moan and looked skyward. "I should have known. You didn't strike me as the typical volunteer we get here."

"Really?" I asked, feigning hurt at my inability to be perceived as a bleeding heart liberal.

"No way. Most of the volunteers here are into counter-culture things, go to poetry readings, art galleries. You look like you'd be more comfortable at a football game with a beer in your hand."

"Close," I said.

"Uh-huh," she said. "So you were spying for the other side."

I shook my head. "There is no other side. My candidate's dead."

"There's Lee Finley." she pointed out.

"Who cares."

Mariah gave a nervous laugh that was louder than it might otherwise have deserved. She looked over at me. "I've been doing this crap for nearly half my life," she said. "I was the Deputy Manager until a few days ago. Kent is scared somebody's going to get too close to the Mayor and threaten his position. He doesn't want anyone else whispering in the Mayor's ear."

"And he pushed you aside," I said.

"With some help," she reminded me, pointing her finger in my direction and then waving a hand. "What the hell. I'm ready for something different anyway. All politicians are the same."

I nodded. "What can you tell me about Mayor Callison that I don't know?"

"You mean why he would like Fairborn dead?"

"That's quick," I said and added, half joking, "you ought to consider police work for your next career."

"I'm not into working for Nazis. Although from what I've seen, working for Callison isn't so great anymore either."

"How's that?"

"We're a pretty liberal community here in Bay City. We allow free lunches to be given away on city property, we don't prosecute the homeless for vagrancy like they do in some communities. We have a progressive way of governing. But I've noticed a change on the part of the Mayor in the last couple of years."

"Meaning?"

"He's allowed a number of major commercial development projects to go through without more than token resistance. Projects that will build the tax base and add money to the city coffers, but it will also change our lifestyle. There's going to be more congestion, more traffic. More people to put it simply, and we're not going to have the resources to adequately serve them. It's a nice community now, but I get the feeling it'll start to look more like New York City in twenty years."

"Why has Callison allowed it?"

"Good question," she said. "He used to be the model liberal. That's why I came to work for him here. I assumed with his reputation, he'd be running for Congress soon, maybe even try for a Senate seat or the State House one day."

"So you wanted to be with him early in his career. Get in on the ground floor."

"Exactly. But from what I can gather, he has no ambition for that."

"Unusual in a politician."

"Isn't it though?" she said. "He seems perfectly content to remain a big fish in a small pond."

I paused for a moment and then cast out the big one. "Do you think he had Wayne Fairborn killed?"

She looked up at me with a frown on her face. "Ordinarily I would say no. I mean, no matter how nasty a campaign can get, killing someone? Unlikely. Especially in a small city like this."

"Unless they have something really big to lose."

"True," she pondered. "Fairborn claimed the Mayor was being backed by real estate interests. Ones that want to tear down the Bay City Airport and put up a business park. And keep building until this place looks like midtown Manhattan."

"How close was Mayor Callison to these developers?" I asked.

Mariah said nothing for a long minute, obviously torn between keeping a confidence and getting even with those who let her down. I often felt revenge was a more compelling emotion than loyalty. Not always more noble, but generally more gratifying.

"Callison received some pretty large campaign contributions from T & R. That's Taylor and Rubin, they're a large commercial development company on the Westside. They're the ones behind Silicon Beach. I heard they're also pushing to develop the area near Bay City College."

"Is Callison on the take?" I asked.

"Not so anyone can really prove," she sighed. "He's accepted some large donations, but it's all on the up and up. Callison's too slick to take envelopes full of cash. Rumor was though, that the other side had something tangible on him. That was a few weeks ago, though. Since Fairborn's death, nothing else came out. Maybe it died with Fairborn."

"So what's next for you?" I asked.

Mariah shrugged. "I don't know. The whole thing is a mess. If I knew Callison would do an about face like this, I never would have come to work here. The only reason I stayed on for this election was to get some experience managing a campaign. Now even that's over. And I'm getting tired of politicians. Callison, Fairborn, they're all the same. Your friend Fairborn wouldn't have been any big change. Just another flavor of sleaze."

"How do you mean?" I frowned.

"He liked to present a goody two shoes image, but I know he slept around."

"No," I said, feigning shock.

"Oh yes," she nodded vigorously. "In fact, he had a thing going on with one of the secretaries at T & R."

I stopped feigning shock. "Does this secretary have a name?"

"Alexa Polo," she said. "I'm surprised you haven't found out. What kind of an investigator are you?"

I winced a little. The kind that would prefer not to squint through peep holes.

*

I went back to Second Chance, waiting a few minutes for Jerry Winkler to finish talking with a disheveled young man about the importance of proper grooming before an interview. The man argued that it wasn't critical how he looked when pushing a broom. Jerry acknowledged that, but told him he'd never get the opportunity unless he showed the employer he believed in cleanliness on a personal level. The young man finally succumbed, and agreed to shave and put on the clean clothes which the Center offered to provide. As the man walked past me, so did the pungent aroma of mildew.

"Hi there," Jerry said. "How goes the master sleuth?"

"I've had better weeks. I sometimes yearn for something simple like an old fashioned missing persons case."

"You don't look so great," he pointed out. "Maybe I should just think of you when my job starts getting me down."

"You try and help people improve their lives. That gets you down?"

Jerry threw up his hands. "This sometimes feels like a never-ending problem. We have thousands of homeless and the trend is increasing. Plus, half the people that apply to Second Chance are just not salvageable. They're psychotic, unstable, and they belong in an institution. Some are alcoholics, some are drug addicts. We're simply not trained to help them."

"Wayne said the problem was more of an economic one. There's always going to be people we can't help."

"Sure," Jerry sighed. "But back when a lot of hospitals lost their federal funding, our society had a choice. We as a community could foot the bill and care for these patients on a local level, or else let them rot in the street. Guess which path we chose?"

I nodded solemnly. "Keeps the tax bills low."

"Most people liked that part a lot. They don't always get the connection between low taxes and things like fewer services. So crime rates go up and taking a stroll in the park becomes a life threatening activity."

"Every action has a reaction," I said, pointing out a basic law of both physics and human nature. "But this is old news."

"Yeah," he said sheepishly. "This whole thing is really perplexing."

"I know. Somebody made a poor attempt to frame you for two murders. That'd mess up anyone's day."

Jerry fingered his wispy blond moustache nervously. "I'm just glad I didn't touch that damn gun. You know, I've put my heart and soul into this job and then some clown goes and tries to ruin my life. I'm wondering why I should come back here tomorrow."

"Because you care," I reminded him. "You're trying to make a difference in the world. And you're doing it."

"So was Wayne. But maybe it cost him his life."

Jerry's argument was valid to a point. If Wayne stayed on as a developer and private citizen, he might well be alive today. He might be happy and he might be perfectly content living a comfortable, materialistic existence. But I felt a part of him would surely be longing for more, a reason to get up in the morning that went beyond seeing how much money he could pile up. Wayne might not have been able to change the world, but he was at least making the effort. Until somebody robbed him of his chance.

"Any idea of who might have slipped the pistol in your desk?"

"None. For all I know it's been there for the past couple of days. I don't even remember going into that drawer. And since the night Wayne was shot, we've been very careful. Nobody gets back here unaccompanied. Rear door stays locked."

"Either it's an inside job," I said, "or there are ghosts at work."

"I may put my money on the ghosts. Only the office staff have keys and I trust them. We don't even allow Eddy up here unaccompanied."

"Whoever planted it had access. Maybe a volunteer."

Jerry shuddered slightly. "I don't even like to consider that possibility. I mean, what's next? Metal detectors at the entrance? We're here to help people and we can't give off the idea we distrust them from the start. These folks are already suffering from serious cases of low self-esteem. I don't think they deserve to be dumped on for the actions of one loon."

"You're right," I said. Jerry needed to provide an aura of trust. But somebody had violated that trust and tried to hang him with it. They were familiar enough to be allowed inside without raising suspicion. Or else had somehow gotten a hold of a key. I wondered why they had targeted Jerry, but why anyone else for that matter? The killer was trying to throw the investigators off the scent, and it may not have mattered who they selected as the sacrificial lamb.

As I got up to leave, Jerry reminded me of the next workshop in two days. I tried to beg off citing a busy schedule, but he reminded me how badly I was needed. Hit me where it hurt.

"With all the publicity lately, it's getting pretty hard to attract volunteers."

It didn't take much arm twisting for me to acquiesce. And I also thought the workshop might attract Mustard, or somebody who knew about him. Besides, the last two events at Second Chance turned up dead bodies and I wanted to be nearby if any more happened to materialize.

I said good-bye to Jerry and went downstairs, no closer to solving this case than I had been yesterday. Or the day before for that. I continued my brooding as I walked to my Pathfinder, when all of a sudden a far more critical concern sprang up.

As I crossed a small side street along Pico, an engine roared simultaneous with the squealing of tires. I stopped in my tracks, which was the worst possible thing to do, but reflex reactions can be arduous to break. A dark colored sports car did a mild fish tail when the engine was gunned, as the weight of the car was unable to sustain the power of the motor. The driver regained control of the vehicle and drove it directly at me. Paralysis gripped me for a split second.

The car was wide and built low to the ground. For a brief instant I thought I could leap high enough so the vehicle would roar under me. Common sense took a stronger hold however, and I bent my knees and tilted my weight onto the balls of my feet. I hesitated for a split second, but upon sensing the driver was not about to stop or swerve, I took a short, quick breath and threw my body towards the sidewalk, away from the oncoming vehicle.

During my years playing safety for USC, the football coaches had us go through a special drill in practice. We would shuffle our feet quickly before diving to the ground and then leaping back to our feet. The idea was to promote quick reflexes and agile, responsive bodies. The drill was physically grueling, but in pads and a helmet I was at least spared from anything but the freak chance of an injury. The fact that we were practicing on a grass field made it safer as well. I thought of this for some reason as my body tore into the asphalt and tumbled into an unyielding curb. The deafening roar of the vehicle closed in and I could literally feel a hot, searing wind glide past. The hideous, noxious fumes poured over me like a thick canopy, as the car narrowly missed its target.

I rolled over onto the sidewalk and scrambled to my feet as rapidly as my body and mind would permit. I needed a couple of seconds to focus and by the time I did, the car, which looked like it might have been a Pontiac Firebird, had sped halfway down the block. The only thing about the driver that was visible was the back of their head. Catching a license plate was out of the question. It took a second for my brain to acknowledge the stinging pain in my arm, as the scraped skin and bruised bones grew agonizing. As I stood there clutching my left arm and regaining my equilibrium, the sound of another set of tires screeched.

A dark grey sedan parked across the street on Pico pulled a U-turn in the middle of traffic, cutting off a number of oncoming cars. The sedan went by me in a flash as they began to tail the Firebird. I only caught a glimpse of the face, but I recognized the strong features and the bulky physique immediately. The intense expression was highly focused. Crystal's father, Serge Markovich, did not look happy.

Twelve

I took my second shower of the day, and afterwards put some topical medication on a nasty scrape above my left elbow. When it dried, I applied a gauze bandage and made a muscle to ensure it adhered. This also served to provide a slight cushion against further irritation, but the stinging was going to persist for a while. I shook my sore wrist a few times. Sprawling to the pavement hadn't done my wrist any good either.

I checked messages and learned Virgil Hairston had called, asking if he could talk to me this afternoon. He was away when I returned the call and I made a mental note to stop by later. After taking a brief respite I trudged out to my Pathfinder. Making a concerted effort to look both ways before crossing the street, I climbed into my SUV and headed back into the late afternoon.

The Bay City freeway turns into Pacific Coast Highway at the McClure tunnel, a narrow, curved, dimly lit structure that makes it tedious to drive any vehicle over forty miles an hour. Once out of the tunnel there are a few dozen beachfront homes that occupy the final boundary of Bay City. Enormous structures, they have housed tycoons and movie stars and even William Randolph Hearst made one of them his West Coast home many years ago. During the Second World War, many of these homes were sold off for a song by terrified owners who thought the Japanese were eyeing the Bay City beach as a landing base for their California invasion. Those who picked up these properties made a lot of money. The only Japanese invasion to actually hit the shore came decades later in the form of raw fish and well made cars.

The Fairborn estate was one of the more august homes, accentuated by a Tudor style design that was as grandiose as it was out of place. The structure was two stories and though the entrance was right on the highway, the home went back at least fifty yards. In the center sat a pool, painted dark blue and shaped like a clam shell. At one of their parties over the summer, I remembered drifting asleep on a chaise lounge chair and the next thing I knew I was being tossed into the pool at Wayne's direction. When I surfaced, he had a mischievous grin on his face.

As I approached the front door I saw Crystal's car, a white Mercedes, parked in the driveway. The car gleamed, except for the driver's door which was scraped and dented. Traces of dark blue paint were evident in the scratches.

The maid ushered me inside and led me into the living room where Crystal sat on a couch, gazing out at the Pacific. The surf was mild, sending soft waves rolling onto the sand and leaving a residue of foam in their bubbly wake. There was a time when I swam regularly in the ocean, but too many sewage spills from the local Hyperion plant had left me with the suspicion that I was doing myself more harm than good.

"Nice view," I commented.

Crystal nodded. "Never changes. The waves keep coming."

"There's a certain security in knowing what's out there," I said.

She turned and looked at me. "I could use some of that. And I appreciate your coming here."

Across the room sat an unused stone fireplace. On the mantle above it sat three dozen condolence cards, most extending sympathy, but one or two wishing a happy birthday.

"Was it your birthday recently?" I asked.

"Wayne's," she said. "Two weeks ago. I haven't felt much like taking them down."

I sat down next to her. "Something happened today. I don't want you to worry, and realistically it doesn't concern you so much as it does me."

"What's wrong?" she asked.

"I went over to Second Chance to speak with Jerry Winkler. After I walked outside, somebody tried to run me over."

Crystal put a hand over her mouth. "My God," she whispered. "Is this ever going to end?"

"It will, believe me. But there was something that happened just afterwards that concerns me almost as much. After the car took off, I saw another car follow it. Your father was driving it. A grey sedan, I believe."

The hand Crystal held over her mouth stayed there a moment longer before she lowered it to speak. "It wouldn't have been a brown car, that was involved, would it?"

I stared at her. "Maybe," I said.

"My father called a little while ago. He was very vague, but he asked if Wayne's brother Peter had a brown colored car. When I told him he did, he wanted Peter's address in Hermosa. I can't understand why Peter would be involved in this."

"Does Peter have a Firebird?"

She shook her head. "I'm not sure."

I rose from the couch. "I better get down to Hermosa Beach and see what's what."

She walked me to the door. "Be careful, Burnside. There's been enough tragedy. I can't take much more."

I felt the stinging in my elbow, the dull ache in my wrist and the soreness around the top of my ear where Bausch's punch had landed the other night.

"Me neither," I told her.

*

A big rig had jackknifed on the San Diego freeway just past El Segundo and traffic was backed up to the Marina freeway. It was stop and go for a long while, and by the time I reached Peter's bungalow, a little over an hour had transpired.

My body tensed as I saw the large grey sedan parked in front of the house. One wheel was on the sidewalk, indicating Markovich had been in a hurry. If there was any good fortune to be garnered, it was that Markovich had likely been tied up in the same traffic jam that delayed me. In the driveway sat a brown MG that bore little resemblance to the Firebird which had come at me earlier.

I ran up the steps and ignored the half dead volleyball that was now sitting near the door. Easing the screen door open I entered the house surreptitiously, moving across the hardwood floor, glad I had on a pair of soft sneakers. Some music was playing in another part of the house. I stepped quietly through the unkempt den before I heard a stirring in the bedroom. Walking in, I saw Peter lying in a heap, blood covering his face. One arm dangled awkwardly at his side as he moaned quietly. He was still alive, but he was losing blood and judging from the head wound needed to reach a hospital quickly.

I drew my gun as I picked up a landline telephone and dialed 911. Speaking in a low tone, I directed the dispatcher to send an ambulance over to respond to a life threatening emergency. I described the injuries as having resulted from an assault, but the situation had been stabilized. A white lie. Paramedics were not allowed to enter a residence if a crime was still in process, and I wanted Peter to receive medical attention immediately. The local police would be notified as well, but paramedics needed to arrive first. The dispatcher asked if I was sure the injuries were life threatening. I took a look at Peter and snarled quietly into the phone that they certainly were and he was losing blood fast.

Hanging up, I moved through the rest of the house, gun drawn, reflexes at the ready. The house was a mess, clothes strewn about, magazines haphazardly opened on the floor. I walked past the den and found the large figure I had expected.

A radio was blaring, apparently the reason why Markovich hadn't heard me. Seated at a desk, he was busy rifling through the drawers. When I flicked on the light to get his attention, he looked up and stared straight into the barrel of my .38.

"Hands where I can see them," I said, approaching him. "Preferably on top of your head."

"What are you doing?" he demanded.

"I'm giving you an order. I suggest you follow it."

He stood up and I reacted by shoving him back down with

my free hand. His massive body bounced as he fell back into the chair.

"You no understand," he said. "I protect you."

"And you no understand. If you don't do exactly what I say, I'm going to shoot you. If my hunch is right, you've just beaten up an innocent man."

He gave me a look that combined both confusion and horror. I patted him down and found him to be unarmed. The thick, barrel chested upper body was solid as a rock. He made no move for the gun and remained frozen while I pawed him for a weapon. The only thing I emerged with was a pocket razor knife, the kind that's used for scraping excess paint from windows.

"Why don't you tell me what's going on here," I suggested. "What were you doing at Second Chance today?"

Markovich cleared his throat. "I try to help you. Why you pull big gun on me?"

I motioned with the gun. "When I hold this gun it means I ask the questions. Now, come on. Give. What were you doing there?"

He looked at me through big brown eyes, his jowls hanging down in a way that made him look like a cartoon character.

"It is true. I follow you. I try to find out who killed my son-in-law."

"Why Peter then?"

"Peter have brown car. It looked like one that almost hit you this morning."

"But it wasn't," I pointed out. "Peter has a little MG. The car this morning was a Firebird. The only thing they have in common is they're both a similar color."

"I no tell difference. I try to follow but it too quick. I know Peter has brown car that look like hot rod."

"I take it you also didn't get the license plate of that car this afternoon."

"No," he said. "But I know Wayne's brother drives sports car. And he no like Wayne. He want Wayne's money."

"That rightfully belongs to Crystal," I offered.

"Yes," he sniffed adamantly, shaking his head up and down. "That right. He no like you investigating."

"He told you that?"

"Yes."

"Before or after you turned his face into chopped meat?"

Markovich squirmed a little in his chair. "I no plan to do this. I just want to talk, but he no let me inside. He call me names. I have to teach lesson."

"Oh you taught him a lesson, all right," I pointed out. "Don't open doors to bulky maniacs unless they're brandishing a shotgun. Peter tell you anything else?"

"He say," Markovich started and began taking rapid breaths, "that my family pack of pigs. That I raise pigs for daughters. Both Crystal and Sara. I no take that from punk like him."

His eyes darted back and forth across the room as he talked. There was something about the manner in which he spoke that was irregular and disjointed. This was a man who had helped build homes for most of his life, and he was now intimately involved in a murder investigation. Something did not fit.

"What were you looking for in Peter's desk?" I asked.

"I look for gun that kill Wayne," he said.

"Gun?" I asked incredulously. "You haven't heard. The gun was recovered. It was planted in one of the offices at Second Chance."

Markovich gave me a blank look. I continued.

"And on top of the fact that you didn't get much information, you may wind up with Peter pressing assault charges against you."

"He no press nothing," Markovich said and raised a big fist. "He know what I do to him next time."

Something snapped inside of me and I reached over and grabbed the big man by the shirt collar. "Listen to me, you dumb son of a bitch. You don't go around beating people up because you think they might be guilty. You need evidence."

Markovich didn't try to resist, he simply listened to what I had to say. I released the grip on his shirt and we stared into each other's eyes for a long minute. I didn't think he was the type to let someone grab him, but after looking into the barrel of a loaded pistol, he may have had some of his machismo tempered. Finally he spoke.

"My wife, she die in car accident many years ago. I have member of my family die in shooting last week. I have nothing but my daughters to live for. I look out for them. I look out for you, too. You watch."

"Don't get in the way anymore," I said, getting exasperated. "I'm warning you."

"All right, I no follow you," he said. "But I find out who did this. You no worry."

The low wail of an ambulance siren interrupted our pleasant chat. I tucked the .38 back into my holster and walked outside, my two hundred sixty pound albatross choosing not to follow me. A red van with lights flashing pulled up in front of the house. Two paramedics got out and I directed them to Peter's bedroom. They asked if the assault was still going on and I informed them the fight was over and they could enter the premises. I didn't tell them who had done the number on Peter, simply saying this was how I found him. The police would get a different story.

I had once read that paramedics ranked second only to fireman in terms of professions that earned the most respect. Both were selfless jobs which gave aid and comfort to those in dire need. The least respected profession was drug dealer, followed by used car salesmen and politicians.

"Is he going to be all right?" I asked, as they worked on him.

"He's lost some blood and he may have a fractured skull," the paramedic said, working rapidly. "I think we got here in time though. I've seen worse and they've pulled through."

The two men moved quickly and efficiently. They cleaned Peter's face carefully and put a bandage over the wound on the right side of his temple. The left arm was placed in a splint and they lifted him delicately onto a stretcher. As they wheeled him out to the van, a Hermosa Beach police cruiser rolled up to the curb. A tall, skinny officer in a khaki colored uniform and wire rimmed sunglasses pulled himself out of the unit and conferred with the paramedics for a moment before he approached me.

"What happened here?" he inquired.

"A man's been assaulted," I said, pointing to Peter. "The other pugilist is inside."

"Who the hell are you?" he peered at me over the sunglasses and revealing a pair of bushy brown eyebrows.

I pulled out my license. "Private investigator."

The cop shook his head. "My lucky day. C'mon show me where this clown is."

As we walked through the front door, a rustling noise could be heard in the backyard. The room Markovich had been sitting in was empty, but the window on the far wall was wide open. A pair of light green drapes blew softly in the breeze. I raced to the window and stuck my head out only to see a bulky figure haul himself over a six foot chain link fence. The fence shook furiously from the weight, and once past the fence Markovich began to move awkwardly through a neighbor's back yard. I spun around and found myself nose to nose with a stone faced cop.

"He's getting away!" I yelled. "Come on!"

The cop pushed me back hard as I tried to run past him. "Nice story, Jack," he sneered.

"What are you doing?!" I screamed. "If we don't move now, the guy who did this'll be long gone!"

"Uh-huh," he said in a voice that was as placid as mine was desperate. "Before I risk my ass, I think you and I are going to have a little chat back at the station house."

My chest began to heave up and down. "The guy who did this..."

"...may be standing right here. You look like you've been through a little brawl yourself today. C'mon Jack. Let's turn around. Hands on top of your head."

Thirteen

The Hermosa Beach jail is hardly a Mediterranean palace, but it is far less intimidating than the Twin Towers facility in downtown Los Angeles. I had the misfortune to be briefly incarcerated there, and it was the closest thing to purgatory I had ever encountered. Aside from the vomit, human excrement and bloodstains that marked the floors and walls, the inmates there were likely to be highly dangerous or certifiably insane. In comparison, Hermosa Beach's jail cell more resembled a cheap motel room with few amenities.

After questioning, the police decided I was the number one suspect and chose to detain me. There were only two people who could corroborate my story and neither would be helping me today -- if they ever would. Markovich was hardly a candidate who would step forward. And Peter Fairborn was still unconscious and in serious condition at Little Company of Mary Hospital in nearby Torrance. That presented a further complication. Should Peter die, I would be looking at a homicide charge.

The cell I was placed in had two beds, a sink and a toilet. It was small and sparse, the grey concrete walls reflecting a cold, barren atmosphere. My roommate eyed me suspiciously as I was led in, his dirty fingers playing with the long grey hair that hung limply down to his neck. Resting languidly on the wafer thin mattress, he propped his head up with a pile of sheets. I spread the skimpy blanket across the other mattress and tossed myself down upon it. A few minutes passed before the grimy man spoke.

"Want a candy bar?" he asked in a gravelly voice. "Two dollars."

I told him no. I had no appetite, and my money and watch had been removed before I was led in. The man reached into his pocket and tossed over a Payday bar anyway.

"Here you go," he said. "You can owe me."

I shrugged and put the candy bar aside for later. I might be here a while. Maybe a lifetime. The thought sent shivers up my spine, and trickles of sweat forming on my brow. When I was imprisoned three years ago it was on a bogus charge also, but the consequences were less serious. And that time I was ultimately sprung on a technicality.

"What are you in for?" the man asked.

I shrugged. "Being in the wrong place at the wrong time."

As if hearing this in slow motion, the man offered a delayed smile after five seconds. His clothes were tattered, but his bright blue eyes had the clear simplicity of a child's.

"Ain't that something," he remarked. "I'm in for the same thing. Where was you sleeping?"

I shook my head. "It's a long story."

"Ain't they all," he agreed. "They busted me down by the Pier. All I was doing was catching some Zs. Not bothering a soul, just having a snooze. Next thing I know, I'm being rousted by one of them brown shirts. If I was ten years younger, I would have cold cocked the son of a bitch."

The man pulled out another Payday bar and peeled the wrapper back. He ate slowly, occasionally smacking his lips and indicating he was garnering much pleasure from the simple act. When the last bite was swallowed, he licked his fingers and sat back peacefully.

"Ain't nothing like a good snack," he declared.

"I thought they normally took all personal possessions. How'd you smuggle those candy bars in?"

"Didn't smuggle them. That jailor knows me, guess he feels a little sorry for me."

I looked at him curiously. Ordinarily I would have preferred to be alone with my brooding and my thoughts. There was something that was both intriguing and scary about the man. He looked ancient, but that was nothing compared to the way I was feeling. I felt old and withered and worn. The future seemed as cold and empty as a winter day in North Dakota.

"What'd you do before you became homeless?" I asked.

"Homeless," he repeated. "They got nice names for it now. We used to call guys that didn't work bums. Or vagrants. Some lady gave me a dollar the other day and told me I was a victim. Imagine that."

I looked at him. "Are you?"

"Victim of my own mistakes, maybe. I'm not gonna lie to you, man. I made myself into what I am. It's my fault."

"What happened?"

"Simple enough story. Had a job for twenty years working as a machinist over in Lomita. The company started having money problems and they finally shipped most of the work to China or India, some place like that. And there was no more room for me."

"You could have gotten another job."

"Man, don't you think I tried? Everybody was letting people go. Nobody hiring. My wife, she supported me for a while but got tired of it. Helen hooked up with another guy, and then I took to drinking, I mean hell, there was nothing else to do. I been on the streets ever since. I'll probably die out there. Or in here. At least in here I get a few meals."

"You can try something else," I said. "I know of a group that tries to help put people back on their feet. You have to want it, though."

"Hell, I want it, sure," he said. "But I'm sixty years old. Nobody'll hire me. It's no use, I've tried. In a couple of years, I can go on Social Security. If I make it that long."

We sat in silence for a while, the only sound being the occasional cursing or yelling that came from a nearby cell. The man's resignation at his fate gnawed at me, and I wondered how I would react to similar circumstances. Clearly, adversity is a true test of a person's mettle. Playing football for USC many years ago left a marked impression on me, and it taught me to never give up hope. Situations change and opportunities have a way of availing themselves to those who persevere. I began to feel a little better, perhaps after considering this man's despair. It's odd how hearing about someone else's problems can lighten your load. My situation was precarious at best, but as long as I had my faculties and a strong body, I wasn't going down without a fight. The world may have its share of quirks and inequities, but life was always evolving.

I slept fitfully that night, but my mind kept spinning and whirring at the dour future that might await me. My thoughts were partially shrouded by the looming possibility of a murder charge. I finally decided to deal with that premise if it arose.

Worrying was one of two useless feelings, the other being guilt. If one takes life as it comes and lives in the present, then worrying about future incidents or feeling guilty about past ones become pointless. This was a lesson I had been trying to remind myself over the years. One of these days it would sink in.

The jailor brought in two trays of food and slammed them condescendingly on the floor. A bowl of oatmeal, a piece of toast and a cup of coffee. My roommate wolfed down his breakfast rapidly, so I offered him mine. I didn't bother to tell him to keep his chin up or to maintain his resolve. He may not have had much to begin with. As he gobbled down the meal, I pulled out the Payday bar and slowly chewed it. My eating habits were becoming as poor as my luck lately.

An hour or so later, the jailor returned to pick up the trays. As he did so, he called out my name loudly, as if there were a dozen people in the cell. I looked at him and said nothing.

"C'mon, c'mon, which one of you is Burnside?"

"If you're here to escort him to the gallows, this Burnside fellow escaped last night."

"You Burnside?"

"Uh-huh."

"You sound like a real jerk," he grumbled and looked down at a piece of paper. "Anyway your release came through. We're springing you."

I got up and stretched my muscles. "What happened?"

"The Fairborn kid regained consciousness earlier. We questioned him and he backed up your story. We're putting a warrant out for that Markovich character. You're free to go. Unless you like it in here, that is."

I shook my head and said good-bye to the old man. He nodded and gave a half-hearted wave. When we were back outside, I signed off for my possessions and handed two dollars to the jailor.

"What the hell's this for?" he asked.

"You mind seeing to it that the old guy gets this? Let's just say I like to keep a clean ledger."

The jailor shrugged and shoved the bills in his pocket. I signed the rest of the paperwork required for my release and stepped back out into the warm California sunshine.

*

Since the Tribune's building was on the way back to my office, I decided to stop off and see Virgil Hairston. As I searched the Trib's parking lot for a space, I noticed his wide body trying to squeeze into a tiny Honda Civic. I tooted the horn twice and pulled up beside him.

"They don't make those cars for your kind of people," I called.

He looked up, surprised. "There's gonna be a law one day that protects overweight folks like me from this type of discrimination."

"Could be," I said. "What's up?"

"His highness, Mayor Callison granted me an interview. In ten minutes. I was hoping to talk to you yesterday so I could get a little more background on what you've come up with."

"Mind if I tag along? I've always wanted to be a journalist. I might also pick up a few things on this case. Think I can pass as a reporter?"

Hairston pondered the thought for a moment. "Why not?" he shrugged, giving me the once over. "You look as grungy as any of us."

We rode over to City Hall in my Pathfinder, and on the way Hairston instructed me to play the part of his assistant. Don't talk too much, hold off on the cynicism, take a few notes, and mostly act like the Mayor is a revered leader.

"In other words," I said, "don't be myself."

"I knew you'd understand."

We arrived at City Hall and were quickly ushered into the Mayor's office. It was a large room with twenty foot ceilings, maple wood floors, and lots of windows facing the ocean. It was the kind of suite one could easily get used to and the Mayor seemed to fit in comfortably here. Jim Callison was a tall man in his late forties, with hair the color of shimmering silver. He had small dark eyes and a nose that was long and sharply angled.

"If it isn't the famous Mister Hairston," he barked, rising to his feet.

"Mister Mayor," Virgil said, walking over and extending a hand. "I'd like you to meet Mister Burnside. He'll be assisting me."

We shook hands. "You look familiar, Burnside. I can't quite place you."

I shrugged. "Do you spend much time in Myrtle Beach?"

"No," he said.

"Me neither. Maybe that's it."

Callison gave me a puzzled look. Perhaps he wasn't used to smart asses. Virgil Hairston interceded at that point and suggested we get down to business. Callison sat down behind his big oak desk and I sank into a hefty leather chair.

"Mayor, I'd like to thank you for granting me this private interview. It's most gracious of you."

Callison nodded appreciatively, as if to acknowledge his place as a fair and just leader. He looked every bit the part of the distinguished public figure: dark tailored suit, white shirt with gold cufflinks and a "JC" monogrammed beneath the pocket. A black and silver club tie finished the look. His face was tanned and his hands had been professionally manicured. He had the tony appearance of a successful actor. The difference between politics and theatre struck me as rather marginal.

"My pleasure," Callison said. "I despise press conferences. The reporters act like barking jackals, and I'm never comfortable enough to get my points across. I really should write my own column in the Tribune. I've been discussing that very issue with your publisher for some time."

"That would lend an interesting perspective, I'm sure," I said diplomatically. Hairston gave me a look and I didn't pursue the thought any further.

"Mayor, how do you look back on your three terms in office? What are you most proud of?"

Callison leaned back and expounded for a few minutes on how Bay City continued to be one of the most livable communities in the area, preserved a high quality of life, and maintained staunchly liberal values in a time where tea party politics were becoming in vogue.

"With the country becoming more conservative, some might say Bay City was behind the times, rather than being progressive," Hairston commented.

"Progressive politics are never out of style. We're here when people are in need."

Hairston scribbled some notes and looked up. "What would you say is the biggest problem facing your office today?"

Callison jutted his mouth outward and raised his head to strike a thinker's pose. After a few moments of careful deliberation, he responded. "Making certain the city runs efficiently."

"Meaning?"

"The citizens only see the final product. They see the nice new buildings, the Third Street Promenade, the movie theaters, the renovation. But all that costs money. Most cities get that through property taxes. But Bay City is a place where renters outnumber homeowners four to one, so it's a real trick to improve things with a limited tax base. We need to get things done using other sources."

"And those sources include..." Virgil asked.

"From the business community."

"So the biggest problem," I chimed in, "is selling the idea of urban growth to a liberal minded citizenry that would ordinarily hate the idea."

Callison lowered his eyelids. "That may be boiling it down too finely. People need to be educated as to the nuts and bolts of what's involved in giving them what they need."

"Or what they think they need," I added.

Callison gave Virgil Hairston a look that asked "who is this guy?" and turned back to me with a stern look. "As a leader, I am keenly aware of what people want. I've been Mayor for twelve years and I listen to what my constituents are saying. But there's a price to be paid for a more upscale way of life."

I raised my hands. "No offense intended."

"It's okay, Mayor," Virgil said. "He likes to get a rise out of people. Don't let it bother you."

The humble servant's terse look was somewhat assuaged. "It's all right," he said and even managed a smile. "I like people with a little spunk. I'm a passionate guy myself."

"Sure," Virgil said. "But since we're on the subject, you've opposed any major commercial or industrial development projects in the past. What changed your position?"

"As I said, the people of the city. Years ago, this was almost something of a retirement community. We had lots of elderly people living here. When they revamped the rent control law, Bay City became more popular with young people, and landlords sought them out. More young professionals began moving in when the elderly ones passed away. They liked the casual lifestyle and the proximity to the beach. But to look around the city, we had too many of these old, tired shops, cheap restaurants and neglected movie theaters. We had to do something to modernize the city and bring it up-to-date with the times."

"What about the problems that come along with that?" he asked.

Callison shrugged. "It's inevitable. It's becoming a bigger, more diverse place, so there's more people coming here. More traffic, more congestion. That sort of thing."

"Crime is higher," Virgil pointed out.

"It's an urban environment now," the mayor spouted quickly, "but on a per capita basis, crime is no higher than it's ever been."

"There are more homeless," he said.

Callison shook his head. "There's more homeless everywhere. It's a societal problem. We're no different than anyplace else. In fact, we take a more humane approach to them here. The homeless aren't prosecuted for vagrancy like they are in some communities. We also work with shelters to help give them a meal, no questions asked. And we don't have a litmus test to make sure they're save-able like that dopey right wing homeless clinic Fairborn was running."

I spoke. "You didn't like Wayne Fairborn much, did you."

"He was my opponent and we naturally had different views on things. And I don't mean to say anything negative about the dearly departed, but I was a lot more honest than he was."

My interest was piqued. When a politician talks about honesty, my first instinct is to put a hand over my wallet. "Why do you say that?"

"I'll tell you why. Fairborn was as big a supporter of development as me," he declared. "Hell, his daddy was one of the biggest developers in the state. That's what made the family fortune. He was just saying he was against further development to win an election he had no business winning."

"But it was working, wasn't it," Virgil said. "The polls showed you guys in a dead heat."

"The election is still a month away. Anything can happen in that time frame. I'll tell you something else about that guy. Fairborn made a lot of noise about helping the homeless in a practical way, helping them get jobs. But the vast majority aren't going to get jobs. They're on the streets because they're either mentally ill or they have substance abuse problems. It's a messy problem, but picking out the few and far between who can be rehabilitated won't solve the homeless problem. No way. I deal with situations as they really are. Patchwork solutions like Fairborn's look trendy and fashionable, but they're not worth a bucket of warm spit."

"That's the vice presidency." I pointed out.

"Huh?" he frowned.

"It's a phrase one of FDR's veeps coined to describe the job. A bucket of warm spit."

Callison looked at me as if I were from another planet. Some people were obviously not fans of trivia. And technically John Garner had referred to the Vice Presidency as not being worth a bucket of warm piss, but I revised that for the sake of manners.

"Uh, Mayor," Virgil said, trying to move on, "how do you feel about Fairborn's replacement?"

"Finley?" Callison scoffed. "He's just like Fairborn, except he doesn't have as much money. He's taking the same stands, same positions as Fairborn. They're clones. Except Fairborn had more dough."

"So you're glad you're facing Lee Finley instead of Wayne Fairborn," I suggested.

"Absolutely not. Lee Finley is a very formidable opponent."

"But you'd rather face him than Fairborn," I said.

Callison pointed a finger at me. "Don't you put words in my mouth, friend."

I looked at the finger and the man behind it. "I wouldn't dream of putting words in your mouth. I'd have to dislodge your foot first."

Callison slammed a fist down on his desk, stood up and

pushed a button next to his phone. "I want you out of here," he said to me and turned to Hairston. "I agreed to this interview as a favor to your publisher. But I'm not going to sit here and take this crap."

I stood up. "We haven't even asked you about Taylor and Rubin yet."

Callison recoiled. "What about them?"

"T & R. They're the ones building that complex over by the Pier. Rumor has it they have another one planned along Olympic."

"I can't comment on that," he said.

"Can you comment why Taylor and Rubin are suddenly your biggest contributors in this campaign, especially since they never made any contribution before. Why hadn't they donated money to your past three campaigns?"

"You need to leave," he said pushing the button under his desk again. And with that, the door opened and in walked his assistant.

"Your next appointment is here, Mayor," she said.

"Gentlemen," he said, "I'm sorry, but I can offer you no further time. I have a very busy schedule. Thank you for coming."

I looked at Hairston and he motioned me to follow. We walked downstairs and out of the building, saying nothing until we reached the street.

"Where were you able to get all that stuff on T & R?" he asked.

"You forget what profession I'm in," I said. "I hope I didn't spoil your interview. I have some trouble heeding requests to speak sparingly."

"That's okay," Hairston said. "That's how people like Callison get thrown off balance. I didn't think you'd pay much attention to my request."

"No?'

"No," he said with a slight smile. "In fact, I was counting on it."

Fourteen

I deposited Virgil back at his office and we promised to keep each other apprised of what ensued in the case. He was still absorbed in the relationship Callison had with Taylor and Rubin, but I only had so much to offer. Local politics was his bailiwick. Mine was solving a murder case. After going home to shower and change clothes, I decided to make up for the time I lost while spending the night in the Hermosa Beach jail.

Alexa Polo's address was plainly listed on the internet. She lived close to the corner of Fourth and Idaho streets, conveniently near my own apartment. Hers was an older building that had seen better days. Some landlords made little effort at repairs. Fortunately for me, my landlord lived in the same building, and if work wasn't performed promptly, he had to endure tenants' gripes on a regular basis. From the looks of Alexa's building, she didn't seem to be as duly blessed.

I rapped on a door whose last paint job may have been completed before I was born. A small black sticker above the lock warned of a security patrol that had gone out of business ten years ago.

"Can I help you?" asked a tall woman in her early thirties as she opened the door. One of these days I planned on providing an honest answer to that question.

I flashed my gold shield that read Private Investigator. "Name's Burnside," I said quickly. "I'm conducting an investigation. I'd appreciate a few minutes of your time."

"Am I in some kind of trouble?" she frowned as she ushered me inside.

"No," I said. "I just need to ask you a few questions. It has nothing to do with all those parking tickets you probably have stacked up."

Alexa laughed a little, softly, and invited me to sit down on the couch. She was about five-nine, slender, and her chestnut brown hair was tied back tightly. She was moderately attractive, except when she smiled and then her whole face lit up. It was a big, wide, engaging, scintillating smile that sent sparks flying. It was the type of smile that reminded me of Gail Pepper's. It was all I could do to focus on the topic at hand.

"I'd like to talk with you about Wayne Fairborn," I said.

Her posture shifted immediately. From sitting daintily at the edge of the sofa, back straight, she stood up momentarily before sinking her lanky body deep into the cushions.

"Oh," she said intelligently, the smile no longer evident.

"I understand you were involved with Wayne."

Alexa took a deep breath. Her mind was concentrating on a memory that made her flinch a few times. "For a short time. A month or two, I suppose. The way it ended, it was, well, a hard chapter in my life"

"That sounds painful," I observed, doing my best psychotherapist imitation. Next I'd be asking who else had hurt her.

"Oh yes," she said, the lilt in her voice making it seem like she were singing the words as much as speaking them. "When you find yourself falling in love with somebody, it's awfully tough to accept the fact that it ends."

"Who ended it?"

She gave me a wistful look. "It wasn't me, I can assure you."

"You loved him."

She sighed. "Of course."

"And did he love you?"

She didn't answer at first, instead choosing to keep her head lowered and her eyes averted. "Oh, I thought he did. He was so sweet and he treated me so special. We really connected with each other. But then, he broke it off very abruptly... it really hurt me. I thought I meant more to him than just a fling."

"Did he say why?"

She gave a sad smile. It wasn't so bright or scintillating any more. "Why does any married man end an affair?" she sniffed. "His wife found out. She demanded he put an end to it. Which he dutifully obeyed. Funny thing, though."

"What's that?"

"I learned later on that I wasn't the first woman he was involved with outside his marriage. God, the more I talk about it, the cheaper I feel. Do we have to continue?"

I nodded as soberly as I could. I wasn't entirely sure where Alexa fit in with this case, but every little bit helped. I had gathered plenty of information on Wayne but there was a central, integral link missing, a piece that might bond everything together. It seemed like a long shot, but I had nothing to lose. Neither did Alexa Polo really, save for a trace of sad reminiscing.

Alexa went over to the kitchen and pulled a bottle of vodka out of a cabinet. I declined her offer, so she took out one tumbler, threw some ice in and followed it with a healthy pour of Absolut.

"I met a woman at the health club not long ago," she said, sipping her drink. "I belong to Sports World over on Centinela. We were riding cycles next to each other and started chatting, and she told me about some volunteer work she did at Wayne's Center, whatever it's called. I knew Wayne so I knew all about the Center. I told her my story about Wayne. She was shocked. Next thing I know she's telling me that *she* had slept with Wayne also."

I shook my head. "What is it about this guy that women find so irresistible?"

"Oh, he's great looking but that's only a part of it. When he's with a girl, he just makes her feel like she's the most special, most cherished thing in the world. That you're the only two people that exist. I know that may sound childish, but there's something wonderful about being protected, being taken care of. It's nice to be around a man who acts like the world's in the palm of his hand."

"Uh-huh," I said. "And the fact that he was married didn't enter into the equation?"

She took another gulp of vodka and stared straight ahead. "Look, it's admittedly not my idea of a fairy tale romance, okay? I'm thirty-one years old and Prince Charming hasn't found me yet. If I meet somebody I'm attracted to and the feeling's mutual, then why not? Maybe I'm selfish that way. Who do we hurt?"

The thought of Wayne's limp body in his chair at Second Chance suddenly flashed before my eyes. I don't know what prompted that vision to loom before me, but it was startling nevertheless. I didn't bother to answer Alexa's question.

"You found out Wayne wasn't Prince Charming."

"Not by a long shot," she said. "And from what I've learned since then, Wayne was notorious for cheating on his wife."

"Did his wife find out about this woman you met at the gym?"

"No. She said she had some sort of a weird connection to him. She said she was the one who ended the affair, and told him it was a one-time thing that could never happen again."

"Do you mind telling me who this woman was?"

She shook her head. "Never got her name. But she felt Wayne had no morals and would sleep with anyone. That there was no woman who would be off limits. That he had no boundaries."

"Did you feel that way also?"

"I don't know. But when he ended it, it was so sudden and finite that I felt used. Used and then discarded, just like a cheap piece of article of clothing. Being abandoned isn't a very nice feeling. One other thing about this woman you might find interesting."

"What's that?"

"She got really mad after I told her about me and Wayne. Said something about taking steps to make sure he didn't do this to another woman again."

*

I thanked her and left. Walking the few blocks back to my humble abode, I started wondering what I had missed about Wayne Fairborn. He struck me as a man deeply concerned and committed to helping people, albeit within his own value system. His relationship with his wife never indicated any outward disenchantment on either side. They were hardly cooing lovebirds, but few long-term marriages maintained a red hot romance forever. There was some issue that was obviously churning beneath the surface of their relationship, apparent perhaps only to the principals themselves. And the lovers Wayne took on.

Perhaps it was the maudlin feeling that exuded from Alexa Polo that made me pick up the phone when I entered my apartment. Perhaps it mirrored my own sadness, and my own sense of isolation and being disconnected from a loving relationship. The vibes I got from the Alexa Polos and Nina Lovejoys and Amy Flanders of the world, attractive, sexy women all, did little to reassure me that everything was right with the universe. Particularly in my own little corner of it.

I had known Gail Pepper for over a year. She was the first woman I had allowed into my life in a long time, my own fears and distrust preventing me from forming any lasting relationship. In the field of law enforcement there is a strong exposure to the seamier side of life, the side which most people never see. Having been on the LAPD for thirteen years, my outlook on life had been colored and jaded. But Gail taught me that not everything was as it seemed. Until she left, I had all but forgotten the void in my life that had existed before her arrival.

I dialed her number and a subdued voice came on the line and said hello.

"Good evening ma'am. I'm conducting a survey on the effect that too many attorneys can have on an otherwise happy, functional society. Would you care to partake?"

Soft laughter floated towards me. "Were you aware you're breaking the law as it currently stands."

"Pardon?"

"The law allows for phone solicitations until nine o'clock in the evening. By my watch, it's a quarter of ten. I believe you're in violation of a federal statute. How do you plead?"

"Usually on my knees," I said. "And with my hands clasped together in a hopeful pose."

"And I'll just bet you look cute that way, *compadre*."

"I wish I could give you an actual demonstration."

"And I wish I could see it."

"I guess we'll have to settle for letting imaginations run amok."

She sighed into the phone. "How are you, honey?"

"Missing you desperately."

"That's good," she said.

"Funny how I have trouble viewing this in a positive light."

"This is a poignant test for us," she said. "We'll see if absence indeed makes the heart grow fonder."

"I'm living proof. What about you?"

"Oh," she said a little too lightheartedly. "I miss you."

"That hardly sounds like a powerful statement," I said, feeling a bit slighted.

"Well, law school eats away most of my time. It's really interesting, but the demands are pretty great. Between classes and reading cases and preparing briefs, my day goes by quickly. I get a lot done, but it's an awful strain sometimes."

My own days were going by rather quickly also, but I was seriously questioning what I was getting done. My accomplishments were a sore wrist, a bruised elbow and the beginnings of a cauliflower ear. Interesting and demanding were words that described my life too, but so were frustrating, disheartening, and physically dangerous.

"If it means this much to you, stay with it," I told her. "Anything good in life is worth working for."

"No matter how much I want to be with you?" she asked.

"It's just a passage," I said. " You heard about Wayne?"

"Wayne? No. What about him?"

"I guess local news down here doesn't travel all the way up to Berkeley. Wayne's dead. Killed by a .32 right through the heart."

Gail gasped. "Oh my God," she said haltingly. "What happened?"

"I'm trying to piece it together," I replied. Without much luck I should add. I went ahead and told her the whole story and included everything I had picked up along the way.

"You know, it doesn't altogether surprise me," she said. "About Wayne's infidelity."

A spark shot through me and it took all the courage I could muster to ask her to expand on that thought. If Wayne put the moves on Gail, I'd be sorely tempted to go and kick over his tombstone.

"He always seemed intrigued by me. And it was more than just friendliness or a passing interest. He had this intense air about him. A sense that everything was important, an event."

"Did he ever make a play for you?" I said, practically choking the words out.

"I swear, you men are the most possessive things," she said, annoyed. "To answer your question, no, he did not. The fact that I used to be a security officer and carried a gun may have played a role in that. Not to mention the fact that you and I are involved. Or you and he were friendly. But it doesn't surprise me that he's played around with other women. Some guys are just always flirtatious."

Heaving a sigh of relief, I managed, "I guess the thought of you with another man doesn't sit very well with me."

I could practically see her gleaming smile across the phone lines. "That's sweet. Old fashioned, but sweet. Next time I see you, I'll have to reinforce this obsession you have with me."

"And when will next time be?" I asked.

"Mmm. I don't know. I might be able to get away for a couple of days. But it may have to wait until Thanksgiving. Unless you'd like to come up here for a weekend."

I smiled. "Am I allowed to be in the girls' dorm after hours?"

"The law is very clear on this," she said. "You're allowed to be wherever I invite you."

Fifteen

I spent much of the next day hunting for Lenny Mast, alias Mustard, who might provide me with some insight into who killed Raff and ultimately who killed Wayne Fairborn. Checking with half a dozen social service agencies and shelters yielded only one person who even remembered him. There was a possibility he might show up at the Second Chance workshop that night, but the way my luck was going, it was likely he'd be elsewhere. I also stopped by Serge Markovich's home in Torrance, but not surprisingly, my knock on the door went unanswered.

The workshop began at seven. Unlike the skeleton crew from the other night, a full host of volunteers showed up for this workshop. Sensing the possibility of Second Chance going under with the demise of its founder, Jerry Winkler got on the phone and rounded up a group of volunteers to work with the twenty or so homeless that arrived. Mustard was not in attendance, but there were plenty of familiar faces nevertheless.

In addition to three new helpers that had attended the orientation last week, this meeting brought out Nina, Mel, Amy, Jerry, and two surprises. I ambled over to them.

"Hello there," I said, as pleasantly as I could manage.

Rusty and Sara Haas looked up simultaneously, as if their movements were connected. In fact, they both began to speak at the same time, and then both paused to give the other the opportunity to talk. Sara finally deferred to Rusty.

"Listen, uh, Burnside," he said. "I'm sorry about what happened last week. It was a bad scene man, and I was out of line. I shouldn't have grabbed you like that. It still bothers me."

I massaged my wrist. "It still bothers me, too."

Rusty managed a weak smile. "Whenever we meet up, somebody seems to get hurt."

"Ain't that the truth."

Sara cleared her throat and I wasn't sure if she was about to speak or about to spit on me.

"How is the investigation going?"

"Not so well," I said, shaking my head. "I'm learning plenty about Wayne, but precious little about who killed him."

"Meaning?" she asked.

"From what I can gather, Wayne was not above a fling or two. Or maybe five or six. He seemed to get around."

Sara looked up at me in amazement. "That's... incredible. How did you find this out?"

I smiled to myself. "We have our ways," I said. "You'd be surprised at some of the things people will offer up."

Sara's mouth remained open. "Who was he with?"

I answered her with the standard company line. "I'm not at liberty to reveal that."

Sara rolled her eyes. "Burnside, does Crystal know about all of this?"

"Some of it. Maybe all of it. I don't know. She hasn't been completely forthcoming with me, but I suppose that when your spouse sleeps around, it's not a topic you really want to advertise."

"Did it," Rusty started, "have anything to do with someone at Second Chance?"

"Someone here tonight?" Sara added. "Like Amy?"

I looked into Sara's eyes, but they revealed little. "Sounds like you know something about Wayne too."

Sara's mouth tightened. "I just know what my sister's told me."

"Maybe we should talk a little about that."

"I don't know if I want to talk to you at all. I don't like the way you speak to people."

"I don't like it myself sometimes," I replied evenly. "But that's often how I learn things."

Rusty put a big hand on Sara's arm and told her to take it easy. Even though Rusty was trying to be the peace maker here, I had an uneasy feeling about him. Rusty's career had faded after our first USC-Notre Dame game, and I knew he held a grudge which was bound to flare up again. But I had the impression he wanted to choose his spot carefully.

"Look, we didn't mean to imply anything," he said. "It's good of you to come by tonight."

"No problem."

"Thank you," Rusty said. "We've been under some strain lately, me being out of work and all. This isn't the best of times for us. That's part of why we're here, to get our minds off our own problems for a little while."

I nodded. "Sure. Other people have issues far worse than most of us."

"That's so true," Sara jumped in, suddenly forgetting she didn't want to speak with me. "I'm also writing an article about some of the clients I've met here. Many of the homeless are actually women. They have some fascinating stories. Heartbreaking."

"I don't doubt that. Speaking of fascinating stories, where do you think I can find your father, the missing Mr. Markovich?"

Sara frowned. "I haven't talked to him for a few days. I suppose he's at home."

I wanted to probe a little further, but Jerry called for everyone to sit down so we could begin. Taking a seat nearby, I listened to Jerry talk for a half hour on how to apply for a job. These were basic, common sense techniques such as filling out an application neatly and not drinking before you rolled out of bed in the morning. One man commented that peanut butter had a peculiar ability to conceal liquor on the breath.

"It only hides the smell," Jerry said. "Your voice may be uneven, your actions may be clumsy and your answers may be slurred. Don't take the risk. You may think you need a relaxer, but you don't. Courage comes from within, not from a bottle or a pipe."

At the end of Jerry's talk, we broke into small groups again and went over some basic principles of job hunting. As the session was winding down, I began asking about Raff and Mustard.

"Big fat guy, you say?" asked a short, man named Eckles, who sported something of a pot belly himself.

"Let's just say, he hasn't missed a meal in a while," I said. "Or a snack."

"Yeah, right." Eckles mused. "I know him. Man groans about the chow down at City Hall but I ain't noticed he's passed any of it up. I don't care if the food ain't got enough this or that, long as it fills my stomach. Mustard thinks he's a chef, but I know what he does."

I frowned. "What does he do?"

"He works over at that Italian place on the Promenade. It's called. DeLoia's. Where all them rich folk go to eat them plates of spaghetti with names you can't even pronounce. He ain't no chef, though. He just cleans up when they're done."

"How long's he been working there?"

Eckles shook his head. "A few days maybe. He was over at City Hall the other day bragging about how this would be his last lunch eating like a head of cattle. Said he'd be eating gourmet food for free now. Told us all about it. Said that restaurant doesn't even put out butter for their bread. They just pour out some olive oil into a dish. Can you imagine? Man, if my mama saw that, she'd be in shock."

The thought wasn't exceptionally appealing, I had to admit. As I was about to ask about Mustard's work hours though, I heard a commotion out in the hallway. A jostling of sorts was audible over the din of the workshop and some shouting followed it. I rose and hustled out of the room.

It seemed like little more than an argument, a lover's quarrel perhaps. The throng of about half a dozen people seemed more amused than concerned. Even when Mel Fenster moved his face within inches of Nina Lovejoy's, the reaction of the crowd of mostly homeless people was one of an event happening, rather than a bout of potential domestic violence.

Nina's cheeks were scarlet and her chest was heaving. She said nothing, just listening and watching Mel throw what might be called a conniption. He screamed at her, berated her as a slut, and told her she had as much worth as a cockroach.

Nina took it all in, let him vent his boiling rage on her, his accusations even referred to a somewhat moody private investigator. As he wound down the tirade he finally asked if she had anything to say for herself. With a rage of her own, she answered his question in a two sentence response that evened the score and then some.

"All you ever wanted to do was screw," she said in a voice that was both quiet and trembling, "And you weren't even good at that."

The crowd let out a whoop that indicated that the verbal contest had been decided game, set, and match. Mel's ears were as red as the shade of Nina's face. His chest heaved up and down for a moment before he reared back and slapped her hard across the face. It was a blow that was nasty enough to send her reeling to the concrete floor.

"Get up, bitch," he screamed. "Nobody talks to me like that! I'll show you what a slut deserves."

He reached down and grabbed her by the hair and started to lift. She let out a shriek and by the time I pushed through the crowd, he almost had her back on her feet. His left hand had a hold of her golden locks and his right was getting set to launch another blow.

I drove my good fist, the right one, into the side of his face, just under his eye. Mel doubled over and let go of Nina, looking up at me in anger. Out of a crouched position he weakly tried to throw a punch, which I fended off painfully with my left hand. Grabbing him by his wrist, I twisted it enough to turn him off balance. I threw another right into the pit of his stomach and could practically hear the air go out of him. His face was contorted with agony.

"I think you owe Nina an apology," I said, applying a little pressure to his wrist. He had an anguished look on his face, but his ego was still intact.

"Fuck you," he said with a grimace.

"That's not a very nice thing to say," I pointed out. Drawing his right fist up with my left hand, I pulled it towards me for a moment and then jammed the fist back into his own face. A few people in the crowd began to laugh. If my own wrist wasn't starting to ache again, I might have joined them.

"I think you should say you're sorry," I told him, shoving the fist into his nose this time. "The sooner the better."

His breathing grew more rapid and I thought I saw a few tears develop in his eyes. Looking down at Nina, holding the side of her face and watching intently, I decided a little more humiliation was in order. I forced him to punch his own mouth this time.

"Okay, okay," he whined. "I apologize. I didn't mean it. Okay? I didn't mean it! Could you let go of me already?"

I released his arm and he spilled onto the floor. After a few seconds of composing himself, he yelled something about seeing an attorney.

Reaching over, I helped Nina up. "Go ahead," I snarled. "And this young lady will charge assault and battery. Your attorney can go visit you at Folsom State Prison."

With the show over, the group began to disperse. Nina appeared shaken but insisted she was all right. While I offered to give her a ride home, she declined but agreed to let me follow her back to her condo in case Mel decided to show up. I trailed her in my Pathfinder as she slowly made her way. After what she had been through tonight, I didn't blame her a bit for driving as if a monster were hiding around every corner. When we entered her condo, she asked if I'd like a drink. The idea didn't sound half bad. I told her I'd take anything that was at least eighty proof. This case was doing wonders for my health.

She took out two tumblers, loaded them to the rim with ice chips from a plastic freezer bag and poured three fingers of Jack Daniels into one glass for me, and one part Jack to two parts Coke in the other for her. Bringing the glasses into the living room, she set the drinks atop coasters on the glass and chrome coffee table and sat primly down next to me.

"I really should be using some of this ice for my face," she said. "Mel really slapped me good and hard."

"Lover's quarrel?"

Her mouth grew taut. "Not on my part. Mel seemed to think differently."

"Judging by your final assessment of his abilities, the two of you had more going on than merely discussing political ideologies."

Nina drew in a breath and was silent for a moment. "I know I told you the other day that there was nothing going on between Mel and myself. I think I was just ashamed of it more than anything. Mel and I had a little fling. Big deal. I'm entitled. I just don't believe in letting the world know my business. There isn't anything wrong with that."

I took a good swallow of whiskey and allowed the stinging fluid to linger on the back of my mouth for a moment before letting it slide down my throat.

"In most cases," I started, "there's nothing at all wrong with keeping certain things to yourself. Your private life is just that."

"You're darned right."

"Except when somebody's murdered minutes after you leave them, and your business card is the first thing that's found, sitting smack dab in their lap. Then things become convoluted and personal issues you believe are nobody's business suddenly become crucial to the case. The only way to figure out what happened is if we have access to all the information."

"But just how is my involvement with Mel relevant at all?"

I sighed. "Mel was a spurned lover, correct?"

She shifted uncomfortably and averted her eyes. "Correct," she said.

"And you were beginning something with Wayne. Therefore, if Mel happened to learn this, don't you think that Mel could have shot Wayne in a jealous rage?"

She shrugged. "Maybe."

"Oh maybe, huh," I rolled back into the couch. "And maybe he could slap you around in public and make a big scene. This guy has a lot of hostility stuffed up inside of him. A lot of rage. I don't think it would have taken much to get him to blow his top."

"I suppose," she said. "You know, after you came by my office the other day, I called Mel and told him I didn't want to see him anymore, even as a friend. He couldn't believe it. His ego is so fragile that one little rejection sent him into a blue funk. He even accused me of going out with you. Which I wouldn't entirely mind."

Luscious as she might be, there were probably no two people more ill suited for one another. I took another gulp of

Jack Daniels. "Maybe we could stick to business for a little while," I said awkwardly.

"What can I do?" she asked. "What is it you want to know?"

"Tell me about the night Wayne was killed. Everything."

She threw up her hands. "We went upstairs, we talked and then I left. There's not much more."

"I said everything. What are you leaving out?"

"Oh hell," she said. "We kissed a little. We embraced. And... oh this is going to sound weird."

"It's all right," I said. "Keep going."

"You probably know this already," she said, her eyes closed, "but Wayne carried a gun around with him for self-protection. It was strapped to his ankle. And I asked if I could play with it. He didn't want me to at first, but, well, I'm good at convincing people to do things. He finally took it out of the holster and I held it for a minute. It was such a rush, I couldn't believe it. I got this feeling of... power. Raw power. It was awesome!"

"Go on."

"Oh, you know, I played with it, pointed it at a few things on Wayne's desk. Then we heard a noise, like somebody else was there. Wayne didn't want anybody to see us together, so he told me to leave through the back entrance. The one that led into the alley."

"What did you do with Wayne's gun?"

"I just laid it down on the desk."

"Did Wayne pick it up?"

"Not that I remember," she said.

"Did you see who else was there?"

She shook her head. "I think someone was in the next office. If they were listening, they heard us kissing and playing around. Do you think Wayne was killed over what we were doing?"

"Maybe. Or maybe that's what they wanted everybody to think. One more question. Did you give Wayne your business card that night?"

"No. In fact, I don't think I ever did. That was another weird thing. Whoever did this must have had my card beforehand. I certainly didn't leave it there that night."

Sixteen

It was nearly eleven by the time I pulled myself away from Nina Lovejoy's offer of one more glass of Jack. As flattering as it might have been to have a sexy, vibrant woman take the initiative, there was still the slight possibility she was the one who killed Wayne. Having sex with a murder suspect was not a good career move. Also, my mind was elsewhere. And as old fashioned as it might be, my heart was elsewhere as well.

I arrived at DeLoia's restaurant and waited a few minutes for the Maitre D' to acknowledge my presence. The restaurant was doing an outstanding business; the tables were all full, and there were still some groups of patrons waiting to be seated. The decor was not unlike some of the newer places in the southland. Hip, sparse, and cool were descriptors that sprang to mind. There were high ceilings, minimalist artwork on the walls, tables barely big enough to contain two plates, and a young clientele that was nothing if not loud and boisterous.

"*Buonsera Signore!*" the Maitre D' finally exclaimed in an accent that was closer to Pittsburgh than Palermo. He was dressed in a black suit, white shirt and a black and gold checked tie. "Will that be a table for one?"

"Actually, I'd like to speak with an employee of yours. His name is Lenny Mast."

The Maitre D' peered into my eyes. "I do not believe we have such an employee."

I flashed my badge quickly. "I'm with the INS. I don't think you want to play games with me. Not unless you'd like your establishment closed down in five minutes."

He took a deep breath and looked around the room. Excusing himself, he walked back into the kitchen for a minute. If there was one thing restaurants in Los Angeles shared, it was the knowledge that illegal aliens were almost invariably employed in their business. The labor was cheap, the people worked hard, and they usually didn't cause trouble. The only point of concern was when a member of the Immigration and Naturalization Service came asking to look at green cards. You never saw workers scurry so fast.

The Maitre D' returned a minute later and said Lenny was on break, and would I care to have a bite to eat to make up for the inconvenience of waiting? Not having partaken in the usual sandwiches at Second Chance, I gladly accepted.

The service I received was befitting a head of state and it was completely enjoyable to be pampered. Eckles was right about the bread being served with a plate of olive oil to dip in, and butter was quickly requested as a replacement. The linguine with clams and mussels arrived with the aroma of garlic wafting delicately from it, and a waiter stood at the ready with a block of parmesan cheese and a grater. A cappuccino and a pistachio *cannoli* rounded out the meal. When I inquired politely about the check, they said don't be silly. I was an important and distinguished guest.

After the final sip of coffee, I was ushered upstairs into what was likely the restaurateur's office where a nervous Lenny Mast sat hunched forward with his hands on his knees. He wore a white t-shirt, white pants, and a dark blue apron that didn't even come close to camouflaging that huge belly. The Maitre D' walked in with me and leaned up against the desk.

"This is a very confidential meeting," I turned to him. "I'll need complete privacy."

The Maitre D' hesitated momentarily, and finally agreed to leave. He shot Mustard a glance, as a reminder perhaps for him to watch what he said. As he closed the door, I turned to Mustard and smiled.

"Remember me?" I asked.

Mustard nodded. "You're with the Center," he said. "You're the guy who helped me get this job. I remembered what you said about being enthusiastic and it really worked. Don't tell me you're going to take it away from me now. You can't do that. I haven't done anything wrong."

"Probably not. But I need to ask you a few questions."

"I'm an American citizen. I may not have my birth certificate on me..."

I held up my hand. "I don't care about that. The INS deal was just a ruse so I could get in here and talk to you."

He frowned. "What for?"

"It's about Raff," I said. "I'm looking into the murders of Raff and Wayne Fairborn. And maybe you can help me."

"Why me?"

"Because there are only a couple of people who were identified as being on the scene at the time of Wayne Fairborn's murder. One was Raff, one was a woman named Nina Lovejoy, and the other was his wife who has a good alibi. I can't talk to Raff, but maybe he confided something in people he knew. You and Raff were pretty good friends, right?"

"I guess so. I mean, once I told him that I had done some time in the can."

"Why was that important?"

"I don't know, but Raff, he kept calling me a political prisoner and insisted I was one of the under trodden, whatever the hell that was. Raff was a smart guy, but he had some goofy ideas about leading the poor masses in a revolt against the rich. I'm not saying I like the way the system has worked for me, but I ain't into plotting no revolution."

"Did Raff talk to you about that night Wayne was killed?"

Mustard shook his head. "You know, aside from political rants, Raff was a pretty quiet dude. He watched people a lot, took everything in, but he didn't offer up much. I saw him a couple days after that shooting, and he said nothing about it. I even asked him what he thought, but all he did was mumble about how the wealthy had it coming to them. He also told me how they was kicking him out of his room on account of his music was too loud. He didn't know where to go. I have a room, so he stored some of his things at my place."

A light bulb flickered on over my head, faint as it might be. "Do you still have his things?" I asked.

"Sure. I wrote a letter to Raff's mother, asking if she wanted any of his personal belongings, but if you wouldn't mind storing them, they're all yours."

"Great," I said, standing up. "I'll stick around until you're off duty. By the way, how do you like your new job?"

"I love it," he beamed. "I'll love it even more when I get my first paycheck."

"What do you do here?"

"Help out in the kitchen, mostly lugging boxes here and

there. Sometimes they let me chop vegetables or help get things ready for the chef. They say in time, they'll let me start cooking a little."

"Terrific," I said, feeling good for the first time in a long while. "Stick it out and you'll get what you want. I mean it. I'm rooting for you."

We shook hands and I walked back out into the restaurant. A very nervous Maitre D' approached me as I walked towards the exit.

"Everything all right?" he asked, the Italian accent long since gone.

"You're in the clear. Mast is a good employee. I think you should be glad to have him. As far as anything illegal going on, well, I don't think you'll have any trouble from me."

"That's very reassuring," he said, visibly relieved.

"There is one thing you should be concerned about," I noted.

"What's that?"

"The olive oil just doesn't cut it," I advised. "Stay with butter."

*

I waited until Mustard got off work at one-thirty, gave him a ride to his room and picked up a duffle bag that had Raff's name stenciled in bold black letters. Mustard offered me a beer, but it had been a long evening already and I passed. On the way home I had to nearly prop my eyelids open with my fingers to keep from crossing into the lane of oncoming traffic. I was fortunate I only lived ten minutes from Mustard's apartment. I was even more fortunate that at this late hour, the roads were fairly empty.

Having had such a filling late supper, I skipped breakfast and took Raff's duffle bag to the office for an in-depth examination. I spread his belongings across the floor and wrinkled my nose at the scent of mildew. Amidst the soiled articles of clothing were a potpourri of books ranging from Karl Marx's *1844 Manuscripts* to Mike Royko's *Boss*. There were ravaged copies of Mother Jones, a few birthday cards, some letters, and a DVD of *Chinatown*. This seemed to be the equivalent of going through someone's attic.

I was glancing through a letter from Raff's ex-girlfriend who sympathized with his losing his scholarship at UCLA, but no she hadn't changed her mind about sleeping with him and didn't think sex would be a proper salvation. As I got to the part where she suggested he seek therapy, the ringing of the phone interrupted my posthumous eavesdropping.

"Burnside, this is Dr. Leary," came the harried voice on the other end.

"Doctor."

"Listen, I don't have much time and my wife's in the next room. Violet has an appointment in a few hours with her personal trainer. I'll give you the address. You can set up your camcorder at the far end of his pool near the diving board. There's some bushes you can shoot discreetly from."

"Sounds like you've done a little snooping yourself."

"I've taken some exercise classes from him, yes, so I know the layout. He always has some young stuff walking around there."

"Doctor, are you sure this is worth it?"

"Damn it, Burnside. I've got to know if she's faithful. A marriage isn't worth much if you even suspect your wife is doing it with somebody else."

To that I agreed. I left Raff's things spread out across my office floor, opening a window to let in some fresh air. Sighing, I wondered if things wouldn't be best served by tossing them into the trash. Noticing some handwritten notes though, I decided it might be worth picking through them further just in case.

Violet Leary's personal trainer was named Randy Hyde and he worked out of a home in Malibu Canyon. Situated about four miles from the ocean, the house sat nestled in a peaceful oasis amidst lush green foliage and chirping birds. I parked my car in an unobtrusive grotto near the road and climbed a trail for a quarter of a mile until I reached the back end of the property. A weather beaten sign warning about trespassing lay withered and torn underneath a nearby tree.

I set up my trusty camcorder near the spot Dr. Leary had recommended. There were some bushes to secure my privacy, but enough room to catch everything that was going on inside of the grounds. A small wooden fence surrounded the perimeter of the property. I focused the zoom lens on a series of outdoor weightlifting benches. Some blue foam mats were laid out nearby, and the large pool and Jacuzzi shimmered invitingly.

It was a few minutes past ten when a muscular man in his early thirties emerged from the house, accompanied by the young Mrs. Leary. Violet was attired in a tight blue leotard that did little to hide her shapely physique. She had long slender legs and walked with the grace and confidence of an elegant dancer. Hyde was wearing a pair of black gym shorts and a loose green tank top that advertised a bar in Ensenada.

They spent the first fifteen minutes stretching and doing some calisthenics. I zoomed in for a few artistic close-ups that also served to establish exactly who the players were, but I occasionally took the liberty of panning the pool area and the bubbling Jacuzzi. Violet lifted a few weights and I was beginning to chalk up the whole adventure as a complete waste of time when the workout took on a new dimension.

As Violet did some arm curls with one of the twenty pound dumbbells, Hyde moved behind her and began to help her complete the last few repetitions. In so doing, he slipped his other arm around her waist and planted it there firmly. Violet seemed to concentrate on the weights, but when she finally placed it back on the ground, Hyde's arm stayed on her hip. He took her by the hand and they did a few pantomime curls before he began to kiss her neck. He placed the other arm around her waist and slowly embraced her torso from behind.

I had to zoom in close before I realized the expression on her face wasn't one of sublime ecstasy, but of a very real fear of being violated. The two struggled for a minute, but Hyde' strength prevailed and he threw her down onto a mat and climbed on top of her. She clawed at his face with her nails but he grabbed her wrists and began to grind his body against hers. Violet let out a primal scream that had nothing to do with sexual exhilaration and everything to do with forcible rape. At that point, my investigative work drew to a close. I jumped over the wood fence in one motion.

My legs ate up the thirty yards between the end of the property and the makeshift gym in a few seconds. The .38

bumped against my left ankle a few times but didn't hinder my movement. Timing my steps properly, I planted my left foot a few inches from the struggling couple and let fly with a vicious kick that caught Hyde full in the face. The force of the blow pushed enough of his body off of Violet, so she was able to squirm out from under him and race behind me. He lay there, partially propped up on one elbow, holding his nose. When he finally regained his senses, he looked up at me.

"Who the hell are you?" he demanded.

"The last person in the world you want to see," I answered.

He started to get up and I reached over with my foot and shoved him back down. We repeated the exercise twice, before he lunged at me and tried to tackle my legs. I stepped back and grabbed him by the hair and delivered two sharp punches to the side of his temple. When I let go of his hair, he fell to the ground like a sack of dirt.

Behind me, Violet Leary stood with her arms wrapped around herself, breathing heavily. Our eyes met and she took a step back.

"What is going on here?" she asked, in a voice that nearly shivered in its unevenness.

"I was about to ask you the same question," I said, pulling my card out and handing it to her. "How long have you been coming here?"

"About a month," she said, squinting at the card in disbelief.

"Has Hyde been your trainer all along?"

"No. A guy named Dan Collins worked with me. But Dan wasn't here today and this creep was going to help me through my workout."

"So you never saw him before."

"Never," she shook her head. "What's this all about?"

Some pieces started to fall into place and I decided to level with her. It felt far easier than continuing the charade. Confidentiality had its limits. I also had another paying client.

"I was hired by your husband," I said, breaking a cardinal rule of investigative work.

"Why?" she demanded. "Does he think I'm having an affair?"

"You catch on quick," I said. "Although it looks like he was trying to set one up for you."

She looked down at the fallen trainer who was beginning to stir. "That son of a bitch. We've been married almost two years and he's worried I'm sleeping with half of Malibu. I can't even look at another man in public without him demanding to know if I'd like to screw them. He's always saying how if I'm given the opportunity, I'd lay anyone!"

I asked a question that was sure to make her feel more comfortable with me. "Have you ever had an affair since you've been married?"

Her eyes glowered. "Would it shock you if I said that I hadn't?"

My eyes searched hers but all I saw was a blazing anger. "I suppose not."

"And would it further shock you if I told you my husband, the fine upstanding doctor, has had a few flings of his own that I've learned about?"

I shook my head. "Nope."

"Well then," she said, her voice starting to crack, "you can tell that paranoid fuck that I've had it with this double standard of a marriage and my lawyer will be on his ass before he can turn around."

I looked at her trembling body, the rage that spewed from her eyes, and the final betrayal that had been bestowed upon her. I probably should have let things go at that point, allowed the legal machinations to take their course. But I was feeling pretty miserable about the Wayne Fairborn case, and wanted to accomplish something this month. The wheels of justice could sometimes be made to turn more rapidly.

"Perhaps you don't have to confront him with that just yet," I told her.

"Why not?" she demanded. "This whole marriage has just stripped my dignity away."

"I might be able to strip some of that from your husband."

"What do you mean?"

"I have an idea for the good doctor to get a taste of his own medicine," I said. "And after we're through with him, he may not be writing any more prescriptions."

Some of the fury in her eyes lessened. I told her I'd be in touch in a few days and walked her to her car. As I made my way through the back yard, I noticed Hyde had come to and had risen to his knees. Disdaining a desire to wallop him again, I grabbed my camcorder and jogged slowly towards the fence.

I returned to the office and called Carl O'Brien of the Bay City Police Department. Ox worked the night shift and I reasoned he was most likely just getting up.

"Ox?"

"Who's this?" came the response.

"Burnside. From the softball league. I was on the Montana team the past few years?"

"Burnside," he said with a little humor in his voice. "I remember you. You're the one who tried to bean me with a pitch after I homered off you. In softball, for crissakes."

"Uh, yeah, that's possible," I said. "In a slow pitch league though, I don't think I did much damage."

"Only to your own team. If I remember correctly, next time up, I whacked another homer."

"Best revenge there is," I said. "Listen Ox, I need a favor."

He laughed a little into the mouthpiece. "Jesus. What do you want?"

I told him about my adventure with the Learys and my plans for the swinging dermatologist. He listened carefully before replying.

"Intriguing," he said. "But we can only set him up for a misdemeanor that way."

"I know. I'm going to try and get the A.G.'s office involved."

"Tell you what," he said, "I know an investigator in their shop and he owes me a few favors. Besides, he'll like this kind of deal. Why don't I grease the skids with him."

"You don't mind?"

"Nah. This is gonna be fun," he laughed. "We're gonna have a blast."

"I owe you. Next season, I'll serve you up another gopher ball."

"Don't worry about it Burnside," he said. "In fact, don't change a thing about your pitching. You're doing just fine."

I drew in a breath. "Nice guy."

Seventeen

Before I could continue my perusal of Raff's mementos, a knock came at the door. The wide body of Virgil Hairston sidled into my office, a newspaper stuffed into his coat pocket. He glanced around the room and grinned.

"Didn't your mother ever chide you for not picking up after yourself?" he asked.

"Doesn't every mother? I just found that ignoring her was the easiest tactic."

Hairston eased into one of the two chairs that faced my desk. He leaned back and crossed his legs in a manner that made him seem like he was at home in front of the fireplace. "You read this morning's paper yet?"

I shrugged. "I just read the fish wrap online. AKA the L.A. Times."

"Well now," he said, "You need to be more up on local Bay City news. I'll have to have one of our telemarketing reps give you a call. With the Tribune's new faster format edition, all you need to see is the two sentence summary under the headline. It's especially made for today's busy private detectives."

"Save the step," I answered dryly. "One of your telemarketers did call me."

"The sales pitch didn't work?"

"Uh, no. It was her first day and she was having a little trouble reading the script her boss wrote out for her. She told me her main line of work was really acting. Couldn't have proved it by me."

"Good help's hard to find," he said, and tossed the local paper on my desk. I unfurled it and read through the lead story, the byline going to Virgil Hairston. The headline read "More Traffic Woes To Plague Bay City Soon!" and the article went on to state that the T & R development company was trying to turn another large chunk of land into a business park. The principals, Jackson Taylor and Maury Rubin, had purchased all but three lots along the Olympic corridor, and were negotiating for the final parcel. The article said nothing about Mayor Callison.

"You've done your homework," I said.

"I had some help," he responded with a smile. "Tell me something. How did you originally learn of T & R's involvement with the Mayor?"

"A disgruntled campaign worker," I said. "Apparently she was a little concerned about the Mayor's change of position on whether the city should continue to pursue commercial development. I learned T & R had been making some sizable donations to Callison's war chest."

"Has she any proof of improprieties?"

"None," I said. "They were all within the letter of the law."

Hairston leaned back in his chair. "After the interview with the Mayor, I went through all the campaign contributions made to Callison, they're a matter of public record. I noticed some big numbers from Taylor and Rubin, but also from a number of other sources. Companies named Lieberman Associates, Griess & Solomon, Carat & Carat. I checked them out and they're all subsidiaries owned by T & R."

"So they've been funneling money to Callison under different names to divert suspicion."

"Right. And most of the land along Olympic is owned by this Carat & Carat group. Let's test your powers of deduction. What do you make of the name? And that's Carat as in gold and diamonds not crunchy vegetables."

I thought a moment. "Carat and Carat. C and C. And R and T. Maybe that's T and R."

"Keep going. You're getting very warm."

"But carat is supposed to measure purity. This whole mess doesn't seem very pure."

Hairston laughed. "It's pure something. Bet on that."

"Hmmm. C-A-R-A-T. Callison, Rubin, Taylor. Callison *and* Rubin *and* Taylor."

Hairston put his hands together and showered me with a brief round of applause. "Bravo," he said. "I'm impressed."

"But there was nothing in the article about this," I pondered. "Or anything about Callison for that matter."

"No connection can be made," he said. "At least none I've been able to find. The corporate officers of the property are listed as Jackson Taylor, Maury Rubin, *et al.*"

"And Callison is the *al*," I surmised.

"That would be my guess too."

"And you need a way to pin the tail on this donkey," I said.

"That's where I'm hoping you can help out," he mused, his eyes looking upward towards the ceiling.

"How's that, pray tell?" I asked.

"Carat & Carat has been trying to buy the last three lots along Olympic for a couple of years, but the owner has been unwilling to sell."

"Who is the owner?" I asked.

"I'm not sure why her name is on the deed, maybe it's for tax reasons, I don't know" he said, smiling broadly now. "But the property was originally purchased five years ago by a fellow named Wayne Fairborn. The current owner is his wife, Crystal."

*

Over the next half hour, Virgil Hairston and I concocted a scheme that sounded foolproof. I called up Jackson Taylor's office and set up a meeting for that evening. Taylor's secretary insisted he was unavailable until seven, so I had a large chunk of time on my hands. The pile of Raff's clothes and papers looked wholly unappealing, so I went over to the gym. Wrapping my wrist tightly, I pumped some iron and pounded the bag for a while. As I climbed into my truck I remembered there was a fellow I needed to pay a visit to. I imagined he'd be happy enough to see me. Considering I may have saved his life.

Peter Fairborn was resting comfortably in the Little Company of Mary Hospital in Torrance. He had a bevy of magazines strewn about his bed, and considering the bandages patching his face and the cast protecting his arm, he seemed in relatively good spirits. Half a dozen rows of playing cards sat precariously on his lap as he tried to finish a game of solitaire.

"You look like you're recovering nicely," I said, walking into the room.

"Hey, dude," he said through a slightly open mouth. "What brings you down here?"

"I didn't think you'd remember me. I was the one who found you the other day. A few minutes after Markovich got to you."

It took a few seconds for him to make the connection. When he did, it revealed a broken smile with two or three teeth missing. "That's right. You're the detective, yeah, okay. They told me you were the one who called for that ambulance."

I nodded. "Sorry I didn't get there a little sooner. Markovich lost his head."

"That's an understatement," he said. "Man, I just opened the door and that big sack of shit grabs me and starts accusing me of stuff. Said I been following people, trying to run down somebody. He even accused me of killing my own brother. I mean, can you believe this asshole?"

"Yeah," I said. "Actually I can."

"It was unreal, I tell you. I don't know what he was looking for, but he wasn't gonna find it at my place. He ought to look closer to home."

"Meaning?"

"His daughter'd be the first suspect I'd have looked at. Crystal's so obvious. After that, there's his son-in-law, Rusty that fat whale."

"Because Wayne wouldn't help them out financially?"

"Yeah, there's that. But Rusty just flies off the handle easily. That's part of why he lost his job at the high school. Some kid mouthed off and Rusty popped him. He's trying to teach discipline to guys on his football team and he has none himself. Ain't that a crock?"

"So that's how Rusty lost his job," I said. "How did you dig this up?"

"Guy I play volleyball with teaches over at East Torrance. He says Rusty didn't belong around kids anyways. Had too much hostility in him. I guess that's okay for a football coach, but you gotta have limits, you know?"

"Is that why you think Rusty killed Wayne?" I asked. "Wayne wouldn't help him out with the money, and Rusty flew off the handle?"

"That'd be my thinking. And Markovich storming into my place fits in real well. If he finds something on me, that takes the attention away from who really did it. They can't fool me."

"Apparently not," I said, wondering what Markovich's true mission in this whole scheme of things really was. It certainly felt like Markovich was doing more harm than good.

"And boy, when we find that big oaf, he's gonna have a major surprise coming to him."

"I wouldn't mind having a few words with him myself." I said. "Are you pressing charges?"

"Sure," he said. "Assault and battery when we find him. But that's just the tip of the iceberg. My lawyer's gonna file a multi-million dollar suit against Markovich. You'll get a share too, when you testify. Damn, am I glad you showed up today. We're gonna make us a fortune!"

I looked at the giddy figure smiling through the broken teeth and the white tape that covered a good part of his upper torso. The kid had spunk, I'd give him that. He had been beaten to a pulp for no discernible reason by an obsessed man on a mission, survived it and he was now out to get some payback. Sharing in the profits wasn't exactly what I had in mind for myself. Throughout the case I had speculated if Peter could have been so bold as to take his own brother's life. I was fairly sure he hadn't, but equally sure I was closing in on who had.

"Look," I said grimly, "I'm not planning to make anything off of your injuries. I just came down to wish you a speedy recovery."

"Wow. Someone in L.A. that passes up free money? You're a fish out of water, dude."

"You're not the first one to have noticed that."

Eighteen

At precisely seven o'clock, I walked through the frosted glass doors of the T & R Management building along Colorado Avenue near Twentieth Street. A while back, this street was filled with auto repair shops, small manufacturing plants and single story warehouses. T & R and a few other developers saw the opportunity to make more money by tearing down the structures and erecting groups of office buildings. The companies that assembled electronic components and desk accessories were being pushed out to make room for the various lawyers, tech firms, and post-production houses that wanted a trendy Westside address. Apparently, this was the future.

The lobby was a plush, shiny vestibule with thick pile burgundy carpeting and lots of chrome trim. The walls were made of a highly polished green marble and held a directory which illuminated the names and suite numbers of the tenants. A few people in jackets and ties walked out wearily as I entered. For a change I fit in with the office crowd, my windbreaker, tan dockers and button-down blue oxford shirt made me look like any other grunt that played with a keyboard all day. The only obtrusive difference was that my left arm, which carried the briefcase, also covered a .38 pistol that fit snugly beneath my arm pit.

I rode up the soft, hushed elevator to the top floor and entered the T & R executive offices. It was quiet as the reception area was vacant and the only noise was the distant clicking of a computer keyboard. I followed the clicks down a long hallway where I found a pudgy man wearing a white shirt with his back to the entrance. The office was dimly lit, the only light coming from a small green shaded desk lamp, and the bright light emanating from the computer monitor.

"Mister Taylor," I said.

The pudgy man turned around. He had brown hair, receding in front, with a stylized auburn beard that had flecks of grey around the chin.

"Yes, I'm Jackson Taylor. You must be Mister Burnside," he said, rising to shake my hand.

"That's me," I said. "Realtor to the stars."

"I know most of the commercial realtors in town," he said, looking me up and down. "Never heard of you before."

"I'm new in town. From up north," I said, not bothering to embellish the point by informing him that up north was Montana Avenue, a few blocks away.

"Uh-huh," he said. "Well, if you've signed up Crystal Fairborn, you've certainly worked pretty fast. We've been trying to purchase those lots over on Olympic for a damn long time."

"The Fairborns are friends of the family," I said.

"Sure. But I think we got us a problem, even still."

"Why?" I asked.

"The Fairborns owned the property. And as I understand it, his little wife was taken into custody as a possible suspect. If she bumped off her husband, it's good-bye to that deal."

I thought back to my conversation with Virgil Hairston. We had plotted this out carefully and Taylor was practically following our script to the word.

"The property was purchased by Wayne," I said slowly, "but he recently put the title in Crystal's name. Tax reasons, I suppose. Maybe it was better for him politically, but the property's hers straight away. No probate, no delays. Even if she was charged, the title is still in her name, so legally it has nothing to do with Wayne. And no charges were ever filed against Crystal and the police have released her. I know Crystal would like to sell off a few assets and move on with her life. Most of what they own is joint and that'll be tied up by the attorneys for a while. She needs some money to live on, and this'll give it to her."

Taylor nodded. "That's just what I wanted to hear. I like doing business with motivated people. I'll tell you, the types we have to watch out for is people like Wayne Fairborn. He used to be a good businessman but ever since he entered politics, it was like dealing with another person. He considered selling to us last year, then backed out because he thought it would hurt him in the election."

"He did seem to change his mind on development," I offered.

"That guy was as two-faced as they come," Taylor sneered. "He told me that if we waited until he got into office, he'd sell me the lots and approve the project quickly. It would be business as usual. He just figured it would be easier to get elected by taking a stand against development. He knew he couldn't beat Callison any other way. Crazy election. Fairborn's practically a Tea Party Republican campaigning against development. And he was running against Callison, a Left-Wing Liberal Democrat who's been pro-growth. Only in California."

"Nobody ever said politics made sense," I said. "So it wouldn't have affected you either way. No matter who got elected."

Taylor shrugged. "We've worked with Callison before, so he's a known quantity. If Fairborn lost, Callison was ready to use eminent domain to take over those lots Fairborn owned. The business park will get built either way."

"So," I joked, "you didn't need to go out and shoot Fairborn yourself."

"Nah," he scoffed. "I mean, I was a little concerned when Fairborn got knocked off that there would be a delay in acquiring those three lots. But I'm not about to kill anyone over a business deal."

"Makes sense," I said and brought up another subject. "Do you know anything about a DVD that was sent to Fairborn a few weeks ago?"

A small smile formed on Taylor's lips. "Not a thing," he said. "At least nothing I can talk about."

"You have a wonderful political posture," I noted. "You ought to run for office some time."

"I'd rather pull the strings offstage," he said. "It's cleaner and safer. I like where I'm at."

"Don't blame you," I said, glancing around the well appointed office.

"So from what you told me, it looks like the wife is ready to deal."

"Sure," I said, hoping he didn't give Crystal a call tonight for verification. "She has no political leanings on development. And who wants to hold onto commercial property that a buyer is willing to pay premium dollar for? It's not like there's sentimental value to a parcel of land that houses diesel engine parts."

"How much does she want?"

"Make us an offer."

Taylor opened a desk drawer and pulled out a file. "Let's see," he said, scanning through some papers. "We offered Wayne four point two million last year. That's still a good price."

"That was last year. Make it four point eight and I'll get her signature," I said, knowing virtually nothing about real estate except that you never accept a first offer.

Taylor shrugged and played with a tiny calculator on his desk. "Maybe we can work that," he said and looked up. "Provided she agrees right away."

"I can talk her into it," I said. "We'll need a formal offer, signed by all the principals. I believe your subsidiary company is called Carat & Carat?"

Taylor peered at me. "You've done your homework," he remarked. "I like dealing with people who know what they're doing. You got it. One thing though."

"What's that?"

"This deal has to be strictly confidential. Nothing's discussed beyond the owners or everything's off. You understand?"

"Mister Taylor, I'm a real estate professional," I said, with some hurt pride. "You can count on me for discretion."

"Okay," he said, nodding his head. "Stop by tomorrow

afternoon and I'll have the offer sheet drawn up. Funny how the ball bounces sometimes. I thought this deal would take a while to get done. Shows you just never know."

I smiled. "Ain't that the truth."

*

I left Taylor's office and headed for home. While navigating up Eleventh Street though, I noticed the car that followed me from Colorado was still right behind me. The bluish halogen headlights had stayed with me through four turns. It was too dark to get a description of the car, so at the next stop sign I waited until they caught up and made a normal left hand turn. From my side view mirror, I could see the car following me. It was a brown Firebird.

I drove a few blocks, keeping my eyes on the rear view mirror as much as on the tree lined street in front of me. There was a near full moon out, so I waited until I reached a street where there were a few broken street lamps. Pulling over to the side of the road I stopped the Pathfinder parallel to the sidewalk and with no cars in front of me. The Firebird cruised past me and parked about twenty yards ahead of my truck. I turned off the headlights, but kept the engine running. Stepping out of the truck for a moment, I waited until the lights went out on the Firebird and the motor had been cut.

There was only one person sitting in the Firebird but it was too dark to make anyone out. If I moved towards their car, they might make a hasty exit. Instead, I pretended I had forgotten something and walked slowly back to the Pathfinder. Opening the door, I quickly moved inside, shifted the transmission and roared down the block. As I reached the Firebird, I screeched my truck to a stop directly adjacent to the Firebird, giving them little more than a couple of inches of room. The driver was stuck, and the wild look in his eye told me he didn't like that one bit.

The car effectively immobilized, the driver rolled out of the passenger door exit and rumbled around the corner. I followed casually in the Pathfinder for two blocks until he made a right turn down a one way street, that would have put me going straight into traffic. I pulled the truck to the side of the road and began to pursue on foot. I was half a block behind but unless he was in good condition, I knew I would eventually wear him down.

I maintained my pace about fifty yards behind, watching the figure lunge ahead, his lanky frame bouncing slightly up and down. I took my strides deliberately, trying to cut the distance between us and keeping him in view. My breathing was deep and rhythmic and I enjoyed the feeling of strength in my legs and chest. I hadn't been running since my jog through Palisades Park a few mornings ago and I was feeling good. After three blocks, I had cut the distance between us to twenty yards. He made another right turn and was obviously heading back to his car. I kicked up my pace another notch and opened my throttle into a dead sprint.

As he was about to turn the final corner towards his car, I tackled him from behind and we rolled over into the street. As we did, he managed to get an arm loose and elbowed me in the face. It caught me in the meaty area just under the cheek and I saw stars for a moment before re-gaining my vision. In that moment, he squirmed out of my grasp and tore down the street again. Angry at letting him get away, I scrambled to my feet and took off after him. He was only ten yards ahead of me, but it was far enough for him to open the passenger door of his Firebird and dive in. I reached the car a few seconds later and was about to drag him out when I stopped dead in my tracks.

Mel Fenster looked up at me, his chest heaving up and down. In his hands was a Beretta nine millimeter handgun. It was pointed straight at my chest.

Nineteen

In titling one of his James Bond books, Ian Fleming paraphrased a famous Japanese poet. He wrote that you only live twice: once when you are born and once when you look death in the face. It was not the first time I had had a gun pointed at me, but the intensity of feeling is always the same.

Mel got out of his car, holding the gun like an amateur, too tightly and too far away from his body. He quivered slightly and the gun wavered, though not enough to move the barrel away from the center of my torso. I raised my hands to the level of my head, which would make it easier in the event I chose to make a move for the gun. It's far easier to lower your hands than it is to raise them, but hopefully it wouldn't come to that. We stared at each other wordlessly for a long minute before I finally spoke.

"That's a nasty looking weapon," I said slowly. "You could do some real damage with that."

"You bet your ass I could," he said. "I could blow you off the face of this planet!"

"Yes," I said. "The operative question however, is why you would want to."

He licked his lips. "I've been waiting for you to make your move."

"I've made lots of moves. Which one is going to affect you?"

"You prick," he sneered. "I know what you've been up to. You've been biding your time waiting to make a play for Nina. And when you do, you're going to get a taste of this!"

"Ah," I said, beginning to see some motivation. "You think I've got it for Nina and because she's rejected you, you're going to get even with whoever wants a go at her."

"Uh-huh."

"And that's why you tried to run me down the other day. Because you think I'm having a thing with Nina. Even though you've never caught me with her, and I've never admitted an interest in that direction."

"C'mon, damn it. She wants you. And you know she's hot."

"Yeah, but that doesn't mean I want her. You've got a lot to learn about what I want. It certainly isn't for a twenty-four year old who thinks life is a candy land with no limits. She's gorgeous on the outside and if I was your age, maybe that's all that would count. But I'm forty years old and I don't look at life quite the same way at this point."

His eyes moistened. "You told Nina I was in love with her! What an asshole you are. I didn't want her to know that. Women treat you like shit when they know you like them!"

Logic like that was difficult to argue with. "I didn't tell her you were in love with her. I told her you said the two of you were going out."

"Well, she took it to mean something else," he said, his voice choking with emotion. "And she ended it with me. And then... then you had to slap me around in front of her. Man, I can never face her again!"

"You knocked her down," I reminded him. "You're twice her size. Anyone would have stood up for her."

"Man, I can't face her again," he repeated, whining. "Or any of those people." He sniffed back a tear and the gun trembled again. It was time to make my move.

In one motion I threw my hands down onto his wrist with enough force to push the muzzle away from my direction. I shoved the handle into his groin area and as he winced, I jerked it upwards and straight out of his hands. Taking a step back, I pointed it at him and ordered him to move away from the car.

"Hands on top of your head," I barked. When he didn't perform this task as rapidly as I'd have liked, I took a step forward and kicked his left ankle with my right foot. He let out a yelp and a pained expression formed on his face. Combined with the long hair and dark complexion, he began to resemble an Apache Indian more than a Bay City businessman.

"Okay, let's start by telling me why you've been following me. If you thought I was playing around with Nina, why didn't you just confront me?"

"I wanted to catch you two in the act," he sobbed. "Then I'd take care of you both at the same time. I know you were over at her place the other night. I watched the whole thing through the window with my binoculars. You're lucky you didn't touch her or I would have been in there like a flash."

"Well you don't have to worry about that anymore because it's not going to happen. Nina and I don't have a thing in common. Never had, probably never will. But why try to run me down?"

He shrugged. "I was angry. You broke us up. First I wanted to just kill your ass right off. Then I figured I'd just wait and catch you with Nina. Then I'd nail you both in the act."

"Uh-huh," I said, not sure of whether to believe him, but I've found men tend not to lie when they have tears streaming down their faces. "What about Wayne Fairborn? You knew he was getting it on with Nina, didn't you?"

Mel shook his head. "Not until after he was dead. I thought Wayne was just getting it on with Amy. I mean, I knew they had split up and Amy was really teed off about it, but I hadn't known he was after Nina. I'd of been the one who plugged him if I knew."

"What do you know about Amy?" I asked, watching him closely.

"She's a nut," he said. "And a whore. I mean, she was pretty psyched about getting Wayne. She had it bad for him and it didn't matter if he was married. I asked her out once. I think the only reason she agreed was to get even with Wayne. Rub his nose in it or something. We went to some campaign fundraiser together and Amy got really wasted on tequila. Thought it would be great fun to scare Wayne's wife on her way home. Damn near killed her. Said I should be glad, because with Crystal out of the way she could have Wayne and I could have Nina. I didn't know what she meant at the time, other than she's got a few screws loose upstairs."

I gaped at him. "Does Amy have an SUV by chance?"

"Yeah," he said. "Dark blue Expedition. How'd you know?"

*

I ordered Mel back into his car and directed him to drive off. I waited until the glowing red tail lights of the Firebird disappeared before walking back to my truck. My final warning to Mel was that while I had no interest in Nina, if I ever caught him following either of us I'd make sure he'd get some jail time. I also reminded him of what he once said. Nina wasn't the only fish in the sea.

There is nothing as awkward as walking around town holding a loaded Beretta. Explaining how I got it to one of Bay City's finest would have been difficult to say the least. I surreptitiously emptied the weapon and tossed the gun into the nearest garbage can, and the ammo into one on the next block.

It took many hours, plus a number of bottles of Blue Moon ale, before I drifted off to sleep that night. I dreamed that I was back in my LAPD uniform but the setting was in the midst of a jungle battle. There was lots of shooting and screaming and explosions, but the scariest part was that I didn't know which side I was on. Anarchy reigned supreme.

I woke with a start at a few minutes before six, when the loud rattling of a garbage can thankfully ended my slumber. I glanced out the window at a homeless woman picking through various cans and bottles scattered throughout the bin. Had I been involved in a more sensuous dream I might have been annoyed, but this was a nightmare that could not have ended quickly enough.

My stomach was growling from lack of nourishment, so I wolfed down some Oreos and a cup of coffee. I normally took better care of myself, particularly in my eating habits, but my life seemed to be in total disarray. I hadn't seen my girlfriend in over a month, I had spent a night in jail, I had gotten into way too many physical alterations and now I was ensnared in the murder case from hell. If things got much worse, my meals might consist of fried pork rinds and glasses of Two Buck Chuck.

Liebross Motors was located along Venice Boulevard, about a mile east of the San Diego Freeway. The dealership was situated on a large lot, ringed by a high black fence with barbed wire wrapped around the tops of the poles. I took a stroll around the block and found what I came looking for. A dark blue Ford Expedition was parked innocently on the street. Looking into the front seat, I saw some women's magazines strewn about, a compact mirror and a few stray containers of lipstick. Bending over to examine the passenger door, I noticed the paint job was uneven and the metal was scratched. Taking out a key, I scraped off some of the top coat of paint and saw traces of white paint. Bingo.

I entered the carpeted showroom and looked around. Amy wasn't there so I looked at the half dozen slick new models positioned strategically in the showroom. The Monroney sticker on the window of a Mustang convertible revealed it cost far more money than I had ever paid for a vehicle. According to the ambitious young salesman that approached me though, lack of money was no object.

"Nobody pays cash anymore!" the kid said. He looked all of twenty-three, and had a gold Rolex watch wrapped around one wrist. "Who can afford to? Everybody I sell to has a monthly plan. We've got the best interest rates in town and we offer one hundred percent financing. That means you don't have to spend a penny of your own money on the down payment."

"That's mighty trusting of you. How do you know I can pay it all off?"

"Listen," he said, "you cut a few corners here and there, you find a way. I can stick you in this baby for a little over seven hundred a month. You make that much?"

I nodded, more amused, than wary. There are some months when an extra seven hundred bucks seemed like a fortune.

"Okay, we set you up in a six year open ended lease, doesn't cost you a penny. And this baby has a Bluetooth, a moon roof and it's all leather. It's loaded!"

"Amazing," I admitted.

"So," he said, taking a breath. "What can I do to sell you this vehicle today?"

"Probably not much," I replied. "Actually I'm here to see Amy Flanders."

"Meh, forget her," he sneered. "I can give you a much better deal, plus I know cars. You'd be doing yourself a favor by doing business with me."

"Sorry," I said. "I bet you'd be steamed if she tried this with one of your customers."

"Bet your ass," he said, walking away. "This is survival, dude. Only the strong make it around here."

Or the sleazy. I found Amy Flanders talking with an elderly couple on the lot, discussing the merits of a black Ford Taurus. Having spent the past five years with a black Pathfinder, I had my own opinion about black vehicles. When clean, they're the sharpest things around, but preserving that gleaming finish was next to impossible. And in hot weather, they're as comfortable to sit in as a toaster oven. Amy, however, told them this was the best Taurus on the lot and someone else was coming by that afternoon with a certified check to purchase it.

If the couple decided right then and there, she'd be happy to hide it away and save it for them. To their credit, the couple decided to defer purchase. Amy shrugged and handed them a business card. Maybe the other buyers would fail to show up, she said. One never knows.

"Business booming?" I asked as she walked over to me.

"Oh, it's you," she said with a dour voice. "No, actually it's been a slow week. The only way to get sales sometimes is to lead these people by the hand. They don't know what the hell they want."

"Spending this kind of money can be a scary proposition for some people," I pointed out.

Amy shrugged and lit a cigarette. "Scary? So's getting up in the morning. You interested in buying something?"

I shook my head. "No. I just wanted to talk with you for a few minutes."

"Oh look, is this about that business up at the Center? Because if it is, I can't help you. I don't know who killed Wayne or that guy Raff, but if it's all right with you, I'd simply like to forget about it, you mind?"

"I'm afraid it's not that simple, Amy. Too much has happened. And you're part of the package, like it or not."

She stared at me. "Just how do you mean?"

"You weren't just volunteering your time out of the sheer charity of your heart. You and Wayne were involved. That is, until his wife learned about it."

"Good heavens," she said, looking stunned. "How did you find out about this?"

"Just doing my job," I said casually. "Did you kill Wayne Fairborn?"

"No!" she cried, her mouth twisting in agony. "I loved him! I had no reason to hurt him!"

"But you had reason to try and run his wife off the road," I answered evenly. "The touch up paint on your truck only covers up the evidence. It doesn't remove it. Nor does it take away an eyewitness to the crime."

"Oh no. It was an accident. I mean, nobody got hurt! There may have been a little damage to Crystal's car but it wasn't severe. And anything can be fixed."

"And you left the scene of an accident."

Amy said nothing, but took a long drag on her cigarette.

"Tell me about the DVD," I continued.

She turned her eyes skyward and blew out some smoke. "Oh God, you know about that, too?"

"Uh-huh. Care to tell me about Jackson Taylor's role?"

"Who?"

"T & R Development Company?" I reminded her.

"I'd rather not get into it," she said hoarsely.

"Would you rather tell it to the police? They might be very interested in what happened along Sunset Boulevard that night. Just because no one got hurt doesn't mean a crime wasn't committed."

She took a deep breath and looked like she was about to spill some tears. "Look. I was approached by those two guys, Taylor and Rubin. They said they knew I was involved with Wayne and maybe we could help each other. They wanted a property from Wayne and he wouldn't sell, I guess because he had taken some sort of political stand against that. They figured the best way to get this property was to convince him to drop out of the mayoral race. Once out of politics, he would have no reason to hold onto the land."

"And your reason for going along?"

"I guess I thought Wayne wouldn't have to worry about how a nasty divorce would affect his image with the voters. He had been talking about divorcing his wife for months, but I've heard that line before. I decided to help him out. This way, I could have Wayne, T & R could have their business park, and we're all happy."

"So they set up a camera and recorded you and Wayne."

"That's right. In one of those sleazy hotel rooms along PCH," she said with a sad laugh. "Wayne liked to go there because he assumed we'd never run into anybody. Taylor hired some guy to set up a camouflaged camera and we just had a blast. Believe me, we put on a show."

"And Crystal found out."

"Yes, they sent it to Wayne but Crystal opened the package. The whole thing backfired. Crystal demanded we stop seeing each other. I don't know what she thought she'd accomplish. He started in with Nina a little while after he broke up with me. I finally figured out Wayne was going to sleep around no matter what. He just couldn't say no when it came to women. It was like he was in a big candy store and he could get lots of free samples whenever he wanted. The guy just had a way about him. He'd never stay faithful."

"But you didn't shoot him."

She shook her head vehemently. "I was talking to people outside of Second Chance the whole time. They'll back me up. Plus, I passed the lie detector test."

"Why did you say Crystal was in the alley, then? Was this just revenge on her?"

Amy sighed. "I honestly thought I saw her coming out of the alley. But again, it was really dark out. I can't be totally sure. It did look like her. And there were a couple of other people, like Nina and that guy Raff who left the building through the alley."

I looked into the moist brown eyes. "If you're lying to me, I'll see to it you're put away for that stunt you pulled against Crystal. The D.A. can sell it as attempted murder. And I'll also make sure that DVD gets a much wider range of distribution than you ever dreamed possible. The internet's a really big place."

She looked helplessly at me, her pink cheeks becoming stained with tears and mascara. "I honestly don't know who shot Wayne. I don't! Please believe me, but I had no use for a dead Wayne Fairborn."

It would be a stretch to believe anything a car salesperson said, but right now I didn't have anything to prove her wrong. In fact, I didn't have anything at all.

"The problem is," I finally said, "that I don't know who shot Wayne either."

"Maybe we never will," she said wistfully.

My soul ached when I heard the words; I was almost ready to accept them. I had unearthed a lot of suspects, many of whom could have had a reason to kill Wayne Fairborn. And the more I dug into Wayne's personal life, the more I was discovering a person I hardly knew. His marriage was a facade and his relationships with women were wholly dishonest. My initial motivation to find Wayne's killer had been based to my friendship with him, and a desire to see justice served. While I would always maintain the need to see a criminal put away, at this stage I was wondering if that would ever happen here. There comes a time when you have to put a case aside if there doesn't appear to be much hope of cracking it. The clock on this one was ticking away.

Twenty

I stopped for an early lunch at the Bay Cities Deli and put away a large Godmother sandwich. It was loaded with Italian cold cuts and I hoped -- without success -- that it would fill some void deep within. Afterwards I walked across the street to a diner and drank some coffee until I felt like going back to work. After the sixth cup and the third dirty look from the stodgy waitress, I tossed five dollars on the table and paid a buck and a half to the cashier.

It was a few minutes past one when I walked into the T & R office. The receptionist was still out at lunch, so I walked down the hall unimpeded to Jackson Taylor's office. A familiar face sat outside his office, pulling papers from a filing cabinet.

"Hi, Alexa," I said. "How's tricks?"

She looked up at me and promptly dropped the file she was holding. "Oh not you again," she sighed. "Must you harass me at work? I didn't get a wink of sleep the other night after you came by. Thinking about Wayne again, oh I really don't want to keep dredging things up."

"Then don't," I said.

"But why are you here?"

"I'm picking up something from Taylor."

She looked down at her desk. "There's nothing here for you. Your name's Bernstein, right?"

"Burnside, actually. And the package may be listed for Crystal Fairborn."

"Oh," she said, lifting a brown manila envelope and thrusting it to me. "I didn't realize you had a new job as a courier."

"And I didn't realize you were a blackmailer."

"What?! That's insane!"

"Is it?" I asked. "Weren't you the one who told Taylor and Rubin about Amy Flanders? The girl they recorded in bed with Wayne in some beachside motel?"

"That's not true!" she protested.

"The hell it's not," I rejoined sharply.

Alexa slumped in her chair and took a deep breath. "You've done some digging."

"Tell me about it."

Alexa gave a resigned shrug. "My bosses own a number of hotels near the beach. One of them was the Sail n' Surf. I was talking with the manager about a month ago; she and I are friendly, and I learned Wayne was playing around again. I was a little irritated, the jerk tells me he would never cheat on his wife after me, and what do you know, there he goes again. I knew about Jackson's connection with Mayor Callison and after I passed this on to him, he and Maury hatched a plan. But I didn't blackmail him. My bosses may have, but I'm no blackmailer."

"Of course not," I sneered. "You just let other people do your dirty work for you."

"Look, the guy hurt me! I wanted to get even. I'm entitled, aren't I? Why should he get off scot free?"

"Looks like he didn't." I snapped.

With that, I tucked the envelope under my arm and left the office. Once I reached my Pathfinder, I shuffled through the documents which confirmed Virgil's hunch. With a little luck, this journalist might win a Pulitzer prize one day.

I drove eight blocks up Colorado and pulled over into the Tribune's parking lot. The difference between the Tribune's office and the T & R office was striking. The furniture, the appointments, even the smells in the air were noticeably older, mustier, and more decayed at the newspaper's headquarters. But all the paper did was inform and educate the public. T & R's charter was a whole lot simpler. Make money. And make lots of it.

Virgil Hairston was in his usual repose, feet up on the desk, computer keyboard on his lap and an empty wrapper of an In-N-Out Double-Double burger crumbled into a ball on his desk. Some people had everything.

"You look like you're having the time of your life," I said. "Not a care in the world."

"Yup," he replied. "I have a steady income, money in the bank, and lots of strange people seem to mysteriously know who I am."

"You're living the life."

"Especially when I want a good table at a good restaurant," he smiled.

"For you, that's either Fat Burger or Roscoe's."

Hairston put the keyboard back on the desk. "Don't insult my religion. Tasty food has helped me through more deadlines and more crises than the man upstairs ever could."

"Keep eating that stuff," I said, "and you'll get to meet him real soon."

Hairston slapped his belly and rubbed. He was a big man, but he wore his weight well. The stomach never hung over his belt, and his clothes were invariably the proper size. Some overweight people deserved the name slobs; Hairston was just a guy who was rather big.

"How'd our plan work?" he asked.

"Like a charm," I said and tossed the offer sheet on his desk. He opened it and quickly looked for the signatures. I knew he found them when his eyes lit up and his mouth broke into a broad grin.

"Pay dirt!" he exclaimed. "There's going to be some changes around here when this hits the fan!"

I sighed. "Who'd have thought that the Mayor himself would be a part owner of a syndicate trying to buy the final piece of land to build a business park."

"And all that stuff he was spewing the other day about it being for the betterment of the city. The only thing getting better was Mayor Callison's bank account."

"So it looks like we won a round," I said. "As Yogi Berra once said, I'd like to thank everyone who made this night necessary."

"Yogi Berra," he pondered. "Rumor had it Yogi used to toss pebbles into the shoes of batters from the other teams. Just to slow them down around the base paths. Easy to do when you're crouched next to them"

I nodded. "And to think people called him dumb."

"Dumb like a fox," he smiled.

"Things are starting to take shape."

"Took a while. But not everything is crystal clear at first."

"Sometimes you just have to wait for the dust to settle."

"Which it has," he smiled. "And which is why I'm a little surprised that you don't look a little happier. This is good news, man! C'mon, smile!"

I did so, albeit weakly. The frustration of the case that would not be solved had been wearing thin on me.

"I'm glad we got something on Callison," I said softly. "Hypocrisy is one thing the world can have a little less of. And with less freewheeling development, we'll have a more livable city. But I got into this mess for one reason. To find out who killed Wayne Fairborn. And I seem to have discovered damn near everything about the guy except for that."

Hairston nodded. "Sometimes the most obvious clues are right under our noses. We just have to step back to focus on them. Don't give up. Everything I've learned about you indicates you're a first rate detective. And you used to be a first rate policeman."

I looked up at him, surprised. "Sounds like you've done some research on me."

"Sure have," he said proudly. "Thirteen years on the beat. For twelve of them you were a model cop. A genuine hero. Till you helped out some girl just a little too much. Judy, I believe her name was."

I stared at him. "You've got it," I whispered.

"They busted Judy, a runaway, for prostitution and to beat the rap she turns you in as her pimp. That about right?"

"Yes," I said, my voice barely audible.

"And the moment they turn her loose, she skips town, figuring they won't be able to make anything stick on you, so there's no harm done."

"Except," I murmured, "to my reputation."

"And to the way you handled your job after that. You began meting out your own brand of justice. Perps that you figured would be out of jail in twenty-four hours got a few extra smacks with the baton. Drug dealers' sports cars got left in the middle of the street with the keys dangling from the lock. And any superior officer that suggested you refrain from this type of behavior got a not-so-friendly retort from that acid wit you so liberally apply."

"I don't deny any of it," I said, rubbing the bridge of my nose. "I regret some things, I guess. I only wanted to help Judy out. Put her back where she belonged, which was going to high school not out on the streets. I've seen what happens to kids that get sent to Juvenile Hall and then to some camp. They bide their time till they're eighteen and they can go back on the street again. I tried to make a difference and got burned."

"Tough one," he said. "One mistake actually cost you a career."

I shook my head. "There were too many rules, too many restrictions for me to stay on the job. That incident didn't change me so much as allow my real attitude to rise to the surface. It's better this way. I can do more for people with my own agency."

"Too bad it took something ugly to show you a better path."

"Such is life sometimes," I said. "You know, it's flattering you went to all that trouble to find out about me. Why'd you bother?"

"Oh," he said, smiling. "I thought maybe writing an article about a modern day Philip Marlowe might be in order here.

Our society is a little short on heroes and your story is compelling. People eat that stuff up."

I thought for a moment. "If you write something about me," I said, "make sure the name is spelled right."

*

I arrived back at my office at half past three and was instantly reminded of what I had left there. The sight of Raff's belongings strewn about my floor was bad enough but now there was a further inducement to assign the remains to the garbage bin. His things were beginning to really smell.

Opening a window to usher in some fresh air, I bent down and began poring through Raff's effects, setting up two piles. One was for books and papers that might mean something, the second pile was for everything else. Clothes, half eaten pieces of food, and an impressive assortment of used chewing gum wrappers were assigned to the latter stack. I bundled that one into some old newspaper and dropped it into an orange dumpster in the alley behind my office.

As Raff was a former political science student, it was no surprise that he had a wide ranging collection of books on contemporary urban issues. Civil unrest, urban riots, and the rise of Communism. There were also books by Plato, Kant, and even a copy of Adolf Hitler's *Mein Kampf,* as well as more mainstream novels by Michener, LeCarre, and that towering literary figure, Sidney Sheldon. Raff's taste was nothing if not eclectic. Since the books themselves didn't smell mildewed, there was no reason to toss them, I would certainly be assured of lots of bedtime reading for quite a while. Even if one of

Raff's kin did ask for his things, I doubted they'd be intrigued by Robert Conot's "Rivers of Blood, Years of Darkness".

Raff's papers included those he had written for school, a diary that unfortunately ended six months before, and a few unmailed letters he had written to his family over some unpardonable sins they had committed years earlier. There was also a birthday card but when I opened it up, it revealed more than birthday wishes. I stopped and shoved everything else aside.

It was one of those cutesy, amusing little cards you could find at any drug store or supermarket. The type of innocent card which no one would pay much attention. The front cover showed a clump of colorful balloons with a little teddy bear saying he was sorry he had forgotten the birthday. The inscription inside indicated that the bear couldn't believe he'd missed such an important event. Below it, a long, handwritten paragraph went into explicit detail about another matter of regret. But the card was neither sent by Raff, nor was it intended for him. It began "Dear Wayne."

After skimming through the more personal message, I found my heart pounding and my breath short. I sat down at my desk and practically collapsed into the soft chair. I read the note two more times, and shook my head at the revelation. The possibility that I could have easily tossed this into the trash without perusing it was unnerving to say the least. After the heart palpitations finally stopped I began to giggle, and then I started to laugh aloud. The pressure and frustration of solving the mystery at Second Chance was fading away. Finally, after going down all the wrong avenues, I now knew who had killed Wayne Fairborn.

Twenty-one

The sight of Barney Sack's corpulent body hunched over a stack of papers was enough to make me smile. Wearing a pair of granny glasses, Sack wrote feverishly, looking up only occasionally to glance at a thick report. He looked like a man working on a serious deadline.

"Catching lots of criminals today, Officer?" I asked.

Sack looked up and let out an exasperated sigh when he saw who was before him. "Budget review," he said. "I just love administrative work."

"Don't we all," I answered. "That's part of the price for having a nice shiny badge."

"You come up here for anything besides to bust my chops? I don't have the patience for it, so say what you came to say. Otherwise I'll let Bausch have another go at you."

"Tell him to wear a cup next time," I said. "And I do have something for you. About the Fairborn case."

Sack put his pencil down. "What?"

Using a handkerchief, I took the birthday card out of its envelope and handed it over to him. My fingerprints were already on the edge of the card, but there was no point in adding to them.

Sack put on gloves and opened the card carefully, read through it, nodded, and pursed his lips together. "So Fairborn was sleeping around. Big deal. It doesn't add up to murder."

"Throw something else into the pot and it certainly does."

"What's that, hot shot?"

"When Wayne was found, there was a business card of a Nina Lovejoy sitting in his lap. Now, despite what you may believe about the reverse psychology angle, it's likely that somebody besides Nina put it there."

Sack held up the birthday card. "The sender of this?" he asked.

"Simple enough to check. Just run the fingerprints on Nina's business card. You already know there are two sets of prints on it. One, of course, belongs to Nina. I'll bet a million bucks the other belongs to the sender of that birthday card. And you know that taking their prints will be a snap."

"So the killer was going to surprise Wayne with a birthday present and..."

"Decided to kill him instead. With Wayne's own gun that was laying on his desk. Nina had already left."

"Okay. But how does Raff get hold of the card?"

"Raff was rummaging through the offices thinking no one was there," I said. "He saw a present all wrapped up and decided to take it, probably not even knowing what the hell it was. Whether he took it before or after Wayne was shot is immaterial."

"Are you sure?" Sack asked. "What was it?"

"A silver engraved pen stand. I saw it when I visited Raff right after Wayne was killed. Apparently he didn't get the significance of Wayne's initials on the base of the stand. When I pointed it out to him, he decided to return the pen stand to Wayne's office at Second Chance."

"And that's when Raff himself got popped."

"Apparently."

Sack held up the card. "Same person, I imagine."

"That'd be my guess," I answered.

Sack slapped a pencil in and out of his hand. "Okay," he said, looking up at the ceiling. "I can have forensics run the prints on this and check it with the business card. If there's a match, we may have something here."

"I appreciate this," I said. "I know you've been told to lay off the case."

"We've just been told not to continue the investigation. That doesn't mean we stop being cops. I may look the other way on some things, but murder isn't one of them. I'll give you a call tomorrow and let you know what's what."

I turned to leave. "You know Barney, all things considered, you're not such a bad guy after all."

Sack shook his head and picked up his pencil. "Coming from you man, you just don't know what that means to me."

I laughed sardonically. "Yeah, I suppose I do."

*

That night should have been one for celebrating, a night for laughing at the idea that there might ever be a case I couldn't crack. Perseverance, asking tough questions, and following through on whatever leads materialized seemed to have finally paid off. A friend's death was about to be avenged, a killer about to be unmasked. I should have been pleased. Or at least satisfied. Or redeemed. But all I really felt was tired and aching and maudlin. I wanted to place my arms around Gail Pepper. I wanted to have a laugh with Wayne Fairborn. I wanted to share this little victory, this discovery of the mystical piece that connected the puzzle. A bottle of beer and a tuna sandwich was not an attractive substitute. Unfortunately, it was the only option there for me.

The next day was Sunday and I took my first respite in weeks. I slept late, watched some football on TV and even started one of Raff's books. I barbecued a rib eye steak on my Weber charcoal grill and after dinner I went out for an early evening jog. It was a pleasurable day and I capped it off by going to bed early. Ms. Linzmeier didn't engage in any nocturnal activities so I slept for nine hours straight. I awoke to a blue sky, the sun shining and the birds chirping. It was a brand new day.

I got out of bed early, showered and drove over to the Ocean Park Cafe. Once inside the swinging screen doors, I looked around for Carl O'Brien and found him sitting at a corner table, finishing breakfast. He was built solid as a rock, hence the name Ox.

"Hi there," I said, parking myself at his table.

"Morning," Ox said, taking a final bite of a pancake. "Want something to eat?"

I shook my head. "I don't have much of an appetite first thing in the morning. Not these days anyway."

"Problems?" he asked.

"Nothing that won't be going away soon," I answered.

"You P.I.'s got it made, I tell you. Make your own hours and you get top dollar. Plus expenses, I should add."

"Yeah," I mused. "It's a hell of a life."

We drove over to the Neudorf Building and rode up the elevator to the tenth floor. I followed Ox down the hallway, past Doctor Leary's office and through a door marked "Sunset Urology Group". We walked through the waiting room and into the doctor's private office. There were two uniformed officers plus a man in a neatly pressed black suit, a technician, and a sexy looking woman wearing a halter top and jeans. Her outfit was tight enough to bounce coins on. Everyone sipped cups of coffee, while the technician finished drilling a hole in the wall.

"How we doing everybody?" Ox boomed. Introductions were made and I poured myself some coffee. The sexy girl and the guy in the black suit were investigators with the California Attorney General's office. She would be the bait, he would slap the handcuffs on. The uniforms were there in case the good doctor decided to make a fuss about things. The technician was there to make sure the evidence was properly recorded. I was there to validate a hunch. Ox was there for the show.

"This gonna be fun!" Ox exclaimed, pacing back and forth.

The male investigator, whose name was Brad, looked up and smiled. "Now there's a man who enjoys his work."

"You betcha," he said with a wink.

"How did you manage to talk the Urology group into letting us use their office?" I asked.

"We lucked out," Ox said. "One of the doctors here came home to find his house ransacked a few months ago. I took the call and as I drove up, I saw the perp leap the hedges. When I collared him, he had about two thousand in cash and a sack full of jewelry. The doc said if I ever had a urinary problem to stop by. This ain't exactly a urinary problem, but you know..."

"It's a lot more fun," joked one of the uniforms. No one disagreed.

The technician finished securing the wires to a closed circuit television and turned it on for a test. We were treated to a shot of an empty examining room containing a chair, rubbing table, basin, and a whirlpool large enough to dangle a pair of legs in. Satisfied things were in good working condition, we settled in for the occupational hazard of detective work. Waiting.

The woman, whose name was Lila, was only able to secure an appointment with Dr. Leary for eleven o'clock. We spent the next three hours swapping war stories, telling jokes, and talking about USC's chances against Notre Dame the following week. There were few things I missed about being in a uniform, but the camaraderie and the bonding made me almost wish I was still carrying a badge.

At five minutes before eleven, Lila departed from our enclave and sashayed down the hall. Her symptoms involved a small rash located smack dab on her *derriere*. Despite Ox's offer, she declined to give him the opportunity to examine the red marker spots on her bottom for authenticity.

After twenty minutes of waiting, the door to Leary's examination room opened and the technician started recording. The image of Lila appeared on the screen before us. She sat down and gave the doctor a big smile. He had no trouble returning it.

"Good morning, I'm Dr. Leary," he said, extending his hand.

"Lila," she said, shaking his hand. "Lila Singer."

The doctor held her hand for a fraction of a second too long. Lila didn't seem to notice, or if she did, kept it to herself. The smile remained pasted on her lips.

"Are you from this area?" he asked.

Lila shook her head demurely and bit her lower lip. "I'm from back east. New England."

"So am I!" he exclaimed. "I went to college at Dartmouth. Beautiful back there. Especially this time of year. The leaves are changing color and you have those wonderful maple logs burning in the fireplace."

"Oh my, yes," Lila purred. "I just miss it so much. And the men have so much more character back there. More intelligent, more masculine. Oh, you're starting to make me homesick!"

Leary smiled and looked down at her chart. "I see that you're single."

"Single and looking," she smiled. "When I meet the right man, I'm going to make him very happy."

"I'm sure he'll be one lucky guy," Leary said, moving a little closer and patting his hand on Lila's bare knee. "So what brings you in this morning?"

"Well, it's a little embarrassing," she said with a slight giggle, averting her eyes from his gaze. "I have a rash on a very, uh, delicate part of my anatomy."

Leary stroked the knee. "Now, now. It's all right. Doctors view everything. There's not much you can show me that I haven't already seen before."

"Well, there's another problem also. I'm not actively employed right now, so I'm concerned about what your fee is going to be."

Leary waved a hand. "We'll work something out. I have a special feeling about you. You're good people, I can just feel it. Why don't you show me your rash."

Lila hesitated for a moment, then smiled in an embarrassed way and stood up. Looking down at her midsection, she unbuttoned her pants and slowly wiggled out of them, hips gyrating provocatively. The doctor's eyes followed her hands and an audible swallow could be heard when her skimpy lavender panties came into view. She turned seductively and lowered her panties to reveal a well constructed set of buttocks, round, smooth and firm. A random series of red dots spotted both cheeks.

Leary's eyes were practically bugging out of his head as he watched Lila turn her posterior towards him and bend over slightly. He put his hands on her rear and poked and prodded, all the while moving in for a closer look. He massaged her bottom for a minute, and Lila slowly began to respond to his touch, sighing and moving her torso slowly back and forth. Looking over her shoulder, she smiled at the doctor and asked him what he thought. Leary licked his lips before answering, but his hands never strayed from the sensuous patch of skin he was busy caressing.

"How often do you go to the gym each week?" he asked.

Lila pondered for a moment. "Four, five times maybe," she answered. "Say, how do you know I go to the gym?"

Leary smiled. "Elementary, my dear. Locker rooms are veritable breeding grounds for bacteria and fungi. Does your bare skin come into contact with a bench or seat, perhaps?"

"Sure, when I change my clothes. Or when I'm sitting in the steam room."

"*Voila,*" he smiled, moving his hands towards the inside of her thighs. "I prescribe you avoid the steam room and make sure you lay out a towel before sitting down on the bench to get dressed. I'll give you something called Loprox. It's a cream you need to apply twice a day. These nasty little things should disappear soon."

Lila frowned. "But is it expensive, doctor? I can't spend much money."

Chuckling slightly, Leary stood up and put his hands around her slender waist. He bent over and kissed the nape of her neck. "Why don't we forget about the fee," he whispered.

"Oh, but you should be compensated for your time, doctor," Lila declared. "Maybe I can pay you in installments?"

Leary pressed himself against her back and began to fondle her breasts. "You can pay me right now," he breathed.

"You mean sex?" she asked in a voice, far louder than need be, considering his ear was inches from her lips.

The two uniformed officers looked at each other and laughed feverishly. Brad stood up and walked towards the door. "Show time's over, guys. Let's take him."

One of the uniforms crossed his legs. "I think we need a little more evidence, don't you?"

Brad looked uncomfortable. "She gave the code. Let's do it."

On the screen, Leary was struggling to stick his tongue in Lila's ear. "Sex?" she yelled loudly. "Is it sex you mean?"

The other uniform took a sip of coffee and smiled. "I thought the code word was prick. She hasn't said prick yet."

Brad opened the door. "It was sex," he insisted. "You guys are a bunch of sick bastards. Now get in there now or I'll see to it you go on report."

The cops slowly stood up. "Now, don't go and stir up trouble. We just need to be sure."

The three of them finally departed for Leary's office and by the time they barged through the door and announced themselves, Leary and Lila were tangled up on the chair. The cops pulled Leary to his feet and jerked his arms behind his back. Lila grabbed her jeans and climbed into them swiftly.

"Where the hell were you guys?" she screamed. "I'm practically getting raped! Didn't you hear me?" She continued to berate them as they led the doctor from the office and read him his rights.

Sitting next to me, Ox proffered a derisive laugh. "She's got a lot of spunk," he said. "I don't half blame the doctor for going after her."

"Except when the state board pulls his license to practice medicine," I said, "he may feel a twinge of regret."

I thought of Violet, his pretty young wife, and the violated look on her face when she learned what her husband was doing. I wondered how many student nurses had received an education of another sort when Leary hired them. From my vantage point, he had done more wounding than healing. The doctor of the skin would soon be taking some rather bitter medicine. Dr. Leary had made plenty of mistakes. His biggest one may have been hiring me.

Twenty-two

I was back in my office for no more than two minutes when the knob of my door turned. I looked up from reading some junk mail to see Crystal Fairborn enter quietly and sit down on a chair facing me. In her hand was today's copy of the Tribune. On her face was an expression one might call perturbed.

"I'm glad to see you're keeping up on your paperwork," she said, "with all the hard work you've been doing."

The cynicism did not become her. "I'm not sure I follow."

Crystal held up the newspaper. The headlines blared, "Mayor Callison to Resign!"

I put the junk mail down. "I haven't read the news today. I guess we'll soon say hello to our new mayor, Lee Finley."

She tossed it on my desk. "Allow me to summarize it for you. The Tribune learned that the Mayor was a major investor in commercial real estate that was about to be developed by a company called Carat & Carat. The only delay was because a few lots still needed to be purchased. The owner, a one Crystal Fairborn, is currently in negotiation with Carat & Carat to sell these lots."

I nodded and said nothing. Crystal continued.

"Well," she said, "I thought that was interesting so I called Jackson Taylor and asked where he got the idea I was going to sell. And he told me my real estate agent, Mr. Burnside, had been negotiating with him. Have you added a realtor's license to your repertoire? I just asked you to look into Wayne's death, not splatter our financial holdings across page one of the local paper."

I shook my head. "I have been working on what you hired me for," I said. "And I'm sorry you're upset. Believe it or not, this all does relate back to my investigation of Wayne's death."

"That's a stretch," she said.

"Admittedly, it may seem so. But were you aware that Taylor and Rubin were behind that DVD you received a few weeks ago? The one with Wayne and Amy? Or that Wayne had turned down T & R's offer to buy those three lots you own along Olympic?"

Crystal's eyes widened. "T & R was involved in the DVD?"

"Yes," I said, not especially wanting to delve further into this topic, but seeing few options. The truth was hard to discuss, and it would not get any easier in the days to come. I had to be candid with her, despite the delicacy of the subject.

"What's more, this was far from Wayne's only affair. I don't know much about the state of your marriage, but believe me, Wayne got around. Amy wasn't his only one."

The icy look she walked in with had begun to melt. Her body, rigid and straight a few moments ago, was now slouched in the chair. Her eyes moistened. I had touched a nerve.

"What you say is true," she finally managed. "I suspected as much for a while. Long before the DVD arrived, Wayne's interest in me, well, waned, I suppose is the only way to put it. Our relations deteriorated. I tried for a long time to pretend nothing was wrong. I was the good wife of a wealthy young man who was trying to make the world a better place. There are a million women who would trade places with me, so I didn't complain. I simply counted my blessings and hoped things would change. Hoping against hope."

"Why do you think Wayne was unfaithful?" I asked.

She bit her lip. "I think it was his way of proving his masculinity. It's so childish, especially for a man who had a public persona of maturity and sophistication. I don't entirely understand it, and believe me I have tried to. I think it was his way of reliving adolescence, of not growing up, of keeping his options open."

"Of trying to live forever?" I suggested.

"Yes."

"By avoiding the adult responsibilities of a monogamous marriage."

"Yes."

I hesitated for a moment. "And did you ever have an affair yourself?"

She shook her head fervently. "No, never. If I did it would have been out of revenge, and in the end I'm sure I would have been the one who would have suffered, not Wayne."

I nodded. "You may be right," I said. "There is something you should know, however. I did find out who was behind your car accident a few weeks back. It was Amy Flanders. She and a guy named Mel Fenster were in her SUV. They followed you home and Amy got the drunken idea to try and run you off the road. I found traces of paint on her vehicle that matches yours. We can press charges against her for attempted murder, or at the very least reckless endangerment. We can verify the scratched paint on your car with the blue paint from Amy's vehicle."

The two of us sat in silence for a while. I crumpled up an advertisement for a take-out Chinese restaurant and winced as I tossed it in the trash. Even the simple act of twisting a piece of paper still irritated my wrist. I started to regret throwing away Leary's card for the orthopedic surgeon.

Crystal finally spoke. "I believe I'd like to put that event behind me. So much has happened since, it almost seems trivial by comparison."

"Whatever you think is best," I said.

She shifted around in her chair. "So you found out Callison was corrupt."

I nodded. "Callison was corrupt."

"And now he's out of office."

"Right. Unlike love, there aren't many second chances in politics. One false step and..." I held out my left palm and flipped it over to signify something falling. "Kaput."

"Did Wayne know about this?" she asked.

"If he did, he kept mum about it."

Crystal took a deep breath and looked down at the floor. "And have you learned anything about who killed my husband?" she asked.

"I believe I have."

Her eyes shot up and met mine. Her breathing stopped. "Who?" she whispered in a hoarse voice.

I shook my head. "Not yet. The police are running some tests. All I can tell you is we should have an answer soon. Maybe today. Maybe tomorrow."

"Can you give me any idea?"

"No," I said. "Not until they're taken into custody."

"Did it have anything to do with T & R? Or the election?"

"No on both counts. And I simply can't tell you anymore. You'll find out soon enough."

I left it at that, and despite Crystal's prodding, I gave her no further information. I wanted to be absolutely positive. There was no margin for error here.

*

At four o'clock I called Barney Sack's office but all I got was a busy signal. One of the nice things about my iPhone was the ability to call someone over and over with the tap of a button. So for the next twenty minutes I let my phone do most of the work. As I was beginning to wonder if the receiver had been taken off its cradle, the busy signal was replaced by a soft ring.

"Sack, here."

"At long last, I've finally gotten through. My but you're long winded, Detective."

"Who the hell is this?" he demanded.

"This is your friendly neighborhood private eye."

"Oh, Burnside. I'm glad you called."

I blinked a few times. "That may be a first," I said. "What've you got?"

"The prints on that birthday card of Fairborn's matches up perfectly with Nina Lovejoy's business card. I think we've got a winner here, but I doubt there's enough evidence to convict on this alone. We'll go ahead with it because you never know what'll come out of the woodwork. A witness would be a help."

"Or a confession," I added.

"They don't come so easy. The days of beating perps with a

rubber hose and shining a bright light in their eyes are over. At least in Bay City."

"I may have an idea. When are you bringing in the suspect?"

"ASAP. The warrant was issued this morning and we're working with the Harbor division at LAPD for a pickup. For all I know it's already done. It's a bitch to figure out who's got jurisdiction in that City Strip area."

"True enough," I said. "I may take a ride down there and see what's what."

"Don't get in the way," he warned.

"No worries. I have one last piece of business to finish."

"And hey, Burnside?"

"Yeah?"

"I didn't think I'd be saying this, but thanks for your help. You do good work."

"Aw, Sack. I'll bet you say that to all the PIs."

The exasperated sigh on the other end of the line was followed by the sharp click of the receiver. I just knew I'd win him over eventually.

I landed smack in the middle of rush hour. The San Diego freeway moved at a snail's pace for almost an hour, nearly double the time it would take in clear traffic. I exited on Crenshaw and it took another twenty minutes to reach that drab green building with the strips of paint peeling from the exterior. A blue Plymouth Fury was parked in front of the apartment, so I knew Rusty Haas was home. The license plate holder read "Go Irish".

I noticed a bulky man with a shaved head walk through the alley and toss a bag of garbage into a bin. It landed with a loud clunk. As he walked back towards the front of the building, I moved into his path.

"Doing a little sprucing up for the little woman?" I asked.

Rusty stopped. "Burnside. What do you want?"

"I want to talk to you. I guess it's my good fortune to get here before the police."

His lips parted slightly. "The police? What are you talking about?"

"C'mon. It's over. They're swearing out a warrant right now. The name Haas is right on it. It's over. You can't run and you can't hide."

"I don't know what you're talking about, but I'm gonna kick your ass but good if you don't get out of my way. You got lucky last time, but I'll box your ears, so help me."

"No you won't," I said and watched Rusty's expression carefully. If I could get him going, I might just get what I needed. "Two people have been murdered and somebody's going to pay. I say it's going to be you."

"Me?! You're nuts! I didn't kill anybody!"

"I say you did. And you're going to spend the rest of your life in jail. You'll rot there. Somebody has to pay."

Rusty's face had turned scarlet and his breath was wheezing through his nostrils. His body was rigid and his fists were clenched. "You're not that tough."

"Try me."

"Man I owe you. I should pound your face into pulp. You cocksucker. First, you ruin my career and now you're trying to ruin my life!"

"You still hold twenty years ago against me?" I asked. "It was a clean hit, Rusty. Fair and square."

"I never played another down of football again after that play. I made freshman all-America and I was on my way to the NFL. You ended that for me, you prick." He stared angrily at me.

It had been an overcast day in South Bend many years ago, cold, with the game outlined against the classic blue-grey October sky. USC had been in a real dog fight with Notre Dame, the lead going back and forth all day. The Trojans were winning 17-13, with two minutes left in the game. The Irish had the ball deep in USC territory, at the fifteen yard line, and were faced with a critical third down and short yardage. Notre Dame lined up as if they were going to run the ball up the middle to get the first down. Our defense was playing in tight to stop the run. But the quarterback motioned rapidly with his arms and began calling an audible, changing the play at the line of scrimmage.

I was at free safety and my job was to be the last line of defense. If anyone got past me it was a touchdown. As the quarterback barked the new play, I saw Rusty move out of his fullback position and began going into motion, trotting laterally across the field. This wasn't supposed to happen. If anything, Rusty would have been the guy to hand the ball off to and run for the first down. Or block for the tailback. And as Rusty moved, I watched our linebackers and none of them reacted. Maybe they didn't see him. maybe they thought someone else would cover him. Maybe they were convinced Rusty was in motion just to get them to spread the field. Open up our defense for a short running play to get the first down. Something felt wrong. It was taking a big chance but I started to drift over and follow Rusty.

The quarterback took the snap, faked a handoff to the tailback and went back to pass. Rusty started running up the field and then switched direction and began moving towards the corner of the end zone. It was a great call, and most of the defense was fooled. Rusty was running a fade route and no one was covering him.

I had lined up about ten yards deep, but began backpedaling at the snap of the ball. When the quarterback went back in the pocket to pass, I took off after Rusty at a dead sprint. The quarterback pump faked and then lofted the ball towards him, aiming for his back shoulder. This meant it would be tough to intercept, but the pump fake meant that Rusty would have to slow down and wait a beat for the ball to arrive. That beat was all I needed.

My back was to the quarterback so I didn't know where the ball was. I had one shot to stop the touchdown, and that was to break up the play and prevent Rusty from catching the pass. I saw Rusty stop and wait while adjusting his body to where the ball was coming. As it fell into his outstretched hands, I lowered my helmet and launched the full force of my body into his rib cage. I don't know if it was pure luck or divine intervention, but I arrived at the exact moment as the football. I hit Rusty hard. Hard enough to dislodge the ball from his grasp and prevent the touchdown. What happened next would change Rusty's life forever.

We tumbled out of bounds, and I landed directly on top of him. But somehow Rusty's knee had become twisted and he landed at a strange angle. His anguished scream was jarring and he kept screaming after I rolled off of him. The trainers came racing over to work on him, but after a few minutes they brought a stretcher out and carted him away. He had torn knee ligaments, and back then the medical technology wasn't able to repair this injury in the same way they can today. Rusty's playing career was over. And when the Irish failed to convert on fourth down, USC had won the game.

In sports, there is an implicit understanding that injuries are part of the game. They are rarely intentional, and even in a long standing rivalry such as USC-Notre Dame, the aim is simply to win. The last thing I ever did on the football field was to intentionally try and hurt another player. I sent Rusty a few letters after the season, extending sympathy. But there was never a response. The USC game turned out to be Rusty's last one in a football uniform.

"It was unintentional," I said to him, as he stood before me, chest heaving. "It was part of the game. I was just trying to win."

"You're a cheap shot artist," he snarled. "You ruined my career."

"It was a clean hit."

"And now you're trying to take away the rest of my life. With some bullshit allegation that I killed someone! You're nuts."

"No I'm not."

"Yes, you are," he growled. "And you're not gonna frame me with some bogus charge!"

I looked around at the dilapidated surroundings. "Jail couldn't be much worse than this. I don't think you're giving up much."

With that he charged me, like a raging bull with smoke streaming out of his nose. He lowered his head and wrapped his arms around my waist but I was ready and clapped my hands on his ears to break the grip. I backed up a few paces to give myself some room, and found myself standing on a patch of grass and milkweed. The turf felt a little soft and I surmised it had just been doused with the sprinklers. Rusty didn't seem to notice.

He came at me again, fists up and anger thundering out of him. I hit him with two left jabs to slow him down and followed with a hard right that caught him on the chin. Stunned but not dissuaded, he continued towards me and flung an overhand left. I ducked under the punch and hit him with a flurry of punches to the midsection and finished with a left hook to the nose. He bent over for a minute to catch his breath. A few grade school kids stood across the street watching in earnest. This was undoubtedly better than TV.

Having regained his composure, Rusty started for me once more, albeit a little more warily this time. We bobbed and feigned at one another for ten seconds before Rusty charged and threw a roundhouse right at my ear. I reached up and blocked it with my left wrist and the explosion of pain I felt shoot up my arm was enough to completely immobilize me. Grimacing at the intense pain, I sensed my body recoil backwards.

The next thing I knew, my face was being pounded savagely and I shortly found myself down on both knees, feeling woozy. I stooped over and drew my arms up to protect my face and head. Rusty grabbed at my arms, trying to separate them. Gathering my reserves, I looked down and saw he was wearing sneakers with cleats, and an idea from a long time ago sprang into my mind.

There is a common misperception among football fans that linemen are not very bright. That the size of a player's body is inversely related to their I.Q. Nothing could be further from the truth. Offensive linemen are often the smartest players on the team. During my sophomore year at USC my roommate was Khaled Hoddap, a big offensive tackle who went on to play pro ball for the New York Giants. Khaled once told me what he did when a defender started playing dirty. He would jam their cleats into the ground and push them over backwards. If they were lucky, they got away with a sprained knee, but it caused them enough pain to make them reconsider whatever nastiness they were dishing out. He said he only used it rarely, but it was very effective when employed.

I jerked my hands out of Rusty's grasp and lowered my head. Grabbing the top of his left foot, I shoved the cleat into the soft ground with my right hand, my left being relatively worthless. I reared back and drove my shoulder into Rusty's fat belly and heard a resounding grunt as the air went out of him. I pushed my left shoulder into his chest, jerking his body up. He tried to maintain his balance but the weight had shifted and the only thing keeping him standing was the left cleat stuck into the terrain. I took care of that last detail with a right uppercut to the jaw that landed with a loud smack.

The blood curdling scream came right after his frame crashed into the ground. The leg was twisted grotesquely as his shoe was still planted firmly in the ground. The piercing screams drew a crowd of people nearby, and dozens more watched from their windows. One woman emerged from the crowd and approached us cautiously. Rusty grimaced and moaned on the ground, his eyes finally focusing in on me.

"You prick!" he howled. "You fucking prick! You tore my knee up again!"

I was panting and tried to catch my breath. "It was self defense," I started. "You came at me and got paid back. When you make a mistake you have to pay."

"Pay? Pay for what?!" he screamed and noticed Sara was now standing over him, a look of shock on her face. "I'm not going to jail! I didn't kill anybody! I didn't kill Wayne! It was Sara! Sara did it!"

"That's hard to believe," I said and started to smile. Sara's mouth opened but no words came out.

"You stupid sonuvabitch!" Rusty continued. "She had bloodstains on her blouse that night, the orange one in her closet. Just check it, I tell you. I'm not taking the fall for her! Let her go to prison! Sara killed that bastard Wayne! She did it!"

I reached over and pulled his cleat from the ground to relieve the pressure. "I know she did it," I said. "And now so does half the neighborhood."

Twenty-three

The paramedics took only a few minutes to arrive, and as usual were far more prompt than the police. Rusty Haas was lifted into an ambulance and driven off; one of the paramedics instructed me to have my own wrist x-rayed as soon as possible. He left an ace bandage for me and I gingerly wrapped it around my wrist. No more brawls for a while. I'd have to rely on my razor wit as a weapon, although history proved that was generally better at instigating a fight than avoiding one.

Sara Haas stood silently by, watching her husband be whisked away. I approached her and we sat down on the curb in front of her apartment building. People milled about, but as far as Sara was concerned, we were the only two people on the face of the earth.

"How did you find out?" she murmured.

"It took a while, believe me," I said. "You were very thorough. When you left Second Chance that night, you exited via the alley so most people wouldn't see you. It was dark. I suppose that's why one eyewitness identified your sister Crystal as being on the scene. The two of you do bear a resemblance."

"That must have been that slut Amy," Sara contended.

I sighed. "She's hardly the only one to have slept around."

Sara froze. "What do you mean?"

"I think you know what I mean."

"I don't sleep around," she maintained.

"That one time with Wayne apparently was enough."

Her cheeks turned a bright shade of crimson. She closed her eyes and whispered something to herself. Looking up at me, she again asked how I found out.

"If it was something you wanted to keep to yourself, you would have," I said. "It was your ugly little secret and it probably should have remained so. You gave Wayne a nice birthday present, I believe it was a silver engraved pen stand?"

"Yes," she nodded solemnly.

"And with it came a birthday card where you talked of wanting to make peace with him. That the brief affair you two had was a mistake and should never happen again. That you felt he belonged with Crystal, and that you hoped you two could put this awful liaison in the past. That you could go on with your lives as if nothing ever happened."

Sara nodded and said nothing. I continued.

"But when you saw Wayne and Nina Lovejoy together that night in Second Chance, you lost control. You shot him out of hatred for betraying your sister again, and out of hatred for betraying you. You despised him because when you lost your home he wouldn't help you. But he would help the homeless to no end. So you shot him with his own gun out of anger and jealousy and betrayal. I'll bet you thought that interlude between you and Wayne was his first extramarital affair."

"He told me it was," she whispered in a voice that was barely audible.

"Well, he lied to you. You weren't the first and you weren't the last. I don't know how many women he's had. But I know I can count you, Amy, Nina, and a woman named Alexa."

"Alexa?" she frowned.

"Yes, in fact you've met her, although I gather it was a rather brief encounter."

"What are you talking about?" she asked.

"Alexa mentioned not only having an affair with Wayne but of having met somebody at her gym, Sports World I think it was, who had a brief fling with our Mr. Fairborn also. She never described you physically, except to say the woman was bitter about the whole event and was looking to extract some revenge. I figured you and Rusty belonged to that gym because I saw the Sports World workout bags in your living room last week. That in and of itself wasn't enough to go on, but combine it with the birthday card and it adds up to a possible motive."

"Knowing Wayne, I'm sure you found many people with motives."

"Oh yeah," I replied. "Too numerous to mention. The obvious ones were political enemies, but they merely engage in blackmail. You can only get so passionate over local politics and money. Love and betrayal stir the beast to a far stronger level. Would you not agree?"

Sara looked down at the gutter and said nothing.

"Amy was abandoned by Wayne when her affair with him was brought to Crystal's attention. But she loved him and if anything, was still holding a candle for him. Alexa loved him too, but seemed more inclined to get on with her life. And Nina was just beginning a new tryst and had yet to be dumped. Her boyfriend Mel Fenster was a possibility, but he was accounted for when the shooting occurred. Most everybody who was at Second Chance that night was accounted for, except for Nina and Raff. Proving you killed Raff will be a bit harder."

"Proving I was even there will be a chore," she said slowly.

"I doubt that. You see, your plan of misdirecting the investigation by placing Nina Lovejoy's business card on Wayne's lap had one major drawback. By doing so, you got your fingerprints on the card, thus establishing your being at the scene of the crime. I imagine you obtained the card from Nina because you did some freelance writing for her magazine, *Tomorrow's Woman*. Dropping it in his lap was a nice touch, but it was also your downfall."

Her shoulders slumped, and a downtrodden look became set in her eyes. I was on a roll so I kept going.

"The only person who could have witnessed the shooting was Raff. You didn't know that at the time, but you found out from Crystal that Raff had taken Wayne's pen stand, the one you left for him. That was the reason you were even at Second Chance that night. To leave him a present. When Wayne and Nina went upstairs, you saw the two of them engage in some passion and discovered your brother-in-law was still playing around, albeit not with you.

"Wayne carried a .32 caliber pistol and I gather he was letting Nina fondle it. When they heard a noise, Nina put the gun down and left through the alley. And thinking there was nobody else there, you walked in and did the job on Wayne. With his own gun.

"When the police questioned and then released you, I guess you figured you were home free. Learning about Raff's involvement scared you enough to do the job on him, lest he say what he might or might not have overheard. You had Raff's keys so you could plant the .32 in Jerry Winkler's desk. But Raff had been scared the police might finger him so he returned the pen stand to Wayne's office. What he didn't return however, was the birthday card with the acknowledgement of your affair with Wayne. All I can imagine is he forgot about it. Then again, nobody knew he had it in the first place. I stumbled upon the card almost by accident, but that's how progress comes about sometimes. If Newton hadn't been sleeping under that apple tree, somebody else might have discovered the Law of Gravity."

Sara nodded. "It's a nice story," she said, her voice showing surprising resilience. "You pieced everything together well. Nicely done. But you still won't be able to tie it to me. All your evidence requires assumptions."

"Except for what I just learned from your husband. Blood stains on your blouse. Forensics can determine whose blood type it is, and wouldn't it be a remarkable coincidence if it was the same as Wayne's?"

At that moment, a grey sedan pulled up, and a looming figure pulled himself from the driver's seat. I stood up and felt for my .38 special, as Serge Markovich approached us.

"Daddy!" Sara squealed. "He knows what happened!"

Markovich's eyes grew dark and he took a step towards me. I went for my pistol and drew it from the holster. Holding it with both hands, I took three paces backwards and directed him to stay where he was. I felt for the trigger with my index finger. Fortunately, Markovich kept his distance.

"You knew about this all along, didn't you?" I queried.

He nodded. "I knew. Whole thing."

"And your way of helping her was to impede the investigation. Or to come up with a viable suspect to point the finger at. That was why you worked over Peter Fairborn and why you were going through his desk. Hoping you could find the slightest trace of evidence to deflect attention from Sara."

"She my daughter. I try to help her."

I shook my head. "Hell of a family, I'd say."

At that point, a pair of Torrance police cars drove up and one of the officers bounced out and ordered me to drop my weapon. Not wanting Markovich to get any brave ideas, I tossed it as close to the cop as possible. It landed a few feet away and clattered towards him.

"It's okay," I called to him, raising my arms. "I'm a private investigator and I'm licensed to carry that."

The cop picked up my piece and walked over to examine my license. "Aw shit. Another damned P.I." he said.

It didn't take long for the police to invoke the warrant and take Sara Haas into custody. After cuffing her hands behind her back, Sara's Miranda rights were read to her and she was taken off in one of the unmarked sedans. Markovich sat down on the curb where Sara and I had been, and sadly watched his oldest daughter being driven off to jail. He looked like a man who was as confused as he was pained. I didn't say anything more to him when I left. He had enough problems.

The last traces of a blood red sunset lingered along the coast as I drove back up to Bay City. A full moon had risen in the eastern sky, but it was only a matter of hours before it would slowly begin to wane again. As I walked upstairs to my apartment, I noticed my door ajar. The Torrance police had returned my .38 and I lifted it out of its holster for the second time in less than three hours. Again clutching it with both hands, I leaned up against the wall and kicked the door open. Wheeling around, I pointed the gun inside. A lone figure stood near the window.

"Hands where I can see them," I yelled.

Gail Pepper turned and raised her arms overheard. She wore a gold sweater that clung to her as if it were form fitted. That and her glistening smile were enough to disarm me.

"I guess you forgot I still have a key," she said.

I lowered my gun and shivered. After all I'd been through, I came dangerously close to shooting the person I loved most in the world. The irony could have been humorous. Instead I felt like collapsing.

"What are you doing here," I managed.

"My classes were canceled tomorrow, and you sounded so low I decided to come down and cheer you up. Surprise, surprise."

"More like shock, shock."

Gail looked me over and then started to laugh. She walked over and kissed me hard on the lips. She then took a step back.

"Is that a pistol in your hand, *amigo*?" she said, her eyes shining. "Funny, I thought you'd be glad to see me."

The End

About The Author

David Chill was born and raised in New York City and educated in the public schools. After receiving his undergraduate degree from SUNY-Oswego, he moved to Los Angeles where he earned a Masters degree from the University of Southern California. David Chill is the author of four novels: Post Pattern, Fade Route, Bubble Screen and Safety Valve, all featuring Burnside, a private investigator and former LAPD officer and college football star.

Post Pattern was a finalist in the St. Martin's Press contest for New Private Eye Mystery Writers. Both Post Pattern and Fade Route have received critical acclaim, and both have spent time on the Amazon.com best seller lists. David Chill currently lives in Los Angeles with his wife and son. If you wish to contact David Chill directly, please email him at: davidchill3214@gmail.com

If you enjoyed Fade Route, then don't miss David Chill's third Burnside novel....

Bubble Screen

Here is a sample of this terrific new mystery...

BUBBLE SCREEN PREVIEW

The first time I met Miles Larson, he looked like he wanted to kill someone.

Even though he was clearly over 70 years old and no taller than 5' 8", Miles had the pugnacity of an angry dog whose territory was about to be violated. His wife Clara stood at his side and maintained a similar repose. On the field, the Trojan Marching Band had begun a stirring rendition of "The Star Spangled Banner." The band was spread out sideline-to-sideline on the grassy floor of the Los Angeles Memorial Coliseum, and their formation spelled out the school nickname, T-R-O-J-A-N-S.

"Hey you two!" Miles shouted at a couple in the next row. He then repeated himself until he got their attention. "Take your hats off!"

The young couple were both wearing dark blue baseball caps with italicized lettering that said "Golden Bears." They looked at Miles as if he were from another planet and shook their heads in disgust. Miles' face became contorted with rage at this disregard for what he obviously considered a simple request.

Storming abruptly over to the couple, Miles verbalized his demand once more, this time with his right hand balled up into a fist. While he wasn't a big man, Miles was solidly built and looked like he had some scar tissue on the back of both hands. As the younger man began to ask who he

David Chill

thought he was, Miles shoved a finger two inches from his nose.

"Show some respect for the flag," he yelled.

At that point I sidled over and tried to get in between them. Usually I'm the one to instigate fights rather than prevent them, but Miles was a potential client and keeping him out of trouble suddenly became my first priority.

"I don't think you all want to get thrown out of here," I pointed out to the couple.

"What is this?" the woman protested. "We didn't do anything,"

"Maybe not," I said, wiggling in between Miles and his new friends. "But all of you will get a security escort out of here and you'll miss the game. It's much easier to just take your caps off for 60 seconds."

"It's a free country," the man responded.

"Shut up!" Miles barked. "Now take those damn things off. This is the national anthem!"

I extended my arm to prevent Miles from getting any closer and then turned back to the couple. "You really want to lose these 50-yard line seats? Really? Over this?"

The couple looked at each other in exasperation and then sheepishly removed their headgear. I sensed Miles was about to blurt out a final quip, so before he could make matters worse I grabbed him by the arm and led him back to our seats.

"Damn Cal people," he grumbled. "I'll tell you something, Burnside. I was ready to clock both of them. The girl, too."

"I had a funny feeling about that."

We returned to our seats to enjoy what was left of the national anthem before sitting down. It was a beautiful November afternoon in Los Angeles. Deep blue sky, a few windswept clouds, and a mild 65-degree temperature. A great day to watch a college football game. Not the type of day one wants to ruin by having an altercation over something silly. That is, unless one has an unyielding view of right and wrong.

Miles and Clara Larson were important people at USC. They were important because they had lots of money and gave lavishly to the university. Owners of a successful business for many decades, they were the epitome of the big donors, and were very loyal to the school. They were treated regally, but as Provost Marshall Hunt had warned me earlier in the week, they were loose cannons in many ways.

"There is no filter between their brains and their mouths," he had said. "Especially Miles. He says what's on his mind and thinks anyone who doesn't like it can go take a long walk off a short pier."

"Thanks for making them my problem," I rejoined dryly.

The Provost had laughed heartily. "Oh you'll do well by them, sir. They'll be great clients for you. They believe someone at their company is stealing from them. And when it comes to taking their money, well, that is the ultimate sin. They view things in very stark, black-and-white terms. The company is called Malco. I made the assumption that with your stellar SC credentials, they'd be eager for your help."

"I appreciate the referral. But if someone's stealing from them, why don't they just go to the police?"

"Oh my, no. They despise anything to do with the

government. And they believe the police are tools of the government. They'd rather hire a private investigator. And who better to help them than a former Trojan football star? It didn't hurt that you and Johnny Cleary played together."

It had been over 20 years since I had put on the cardinal and gold uniform, but for some people, my image remained frozen in time. And now that Johnny Cleary had been elevated to head coach of the football team, my status in the Trojan community had only grown. USC had a close knit relationship with its alumni, and maintaining its heritage was very important to the school.

As the band left the field and made way for the teams to line up for the opening kickoff, I turned to Clara. "Does he always get this way?" I asked.

Clara threw her head back and cackled. "Oh sure. He's been tossed out of here a number of times. But he always gets back in once security recognizes who he is."

Having lots of money can help open doors, including the gates at an athletic event. In Los Angeles there were many tiers of wealth, and the Larsons appeared to be somewhere near the upper level. But wealth could be an illusion. The Larsons were not what you would call aristocratic. People who rose to that station in life often employed others to take care of their problems. The Larsons, on the other hand, seemed to delight in a good, old-fashioned confrontation. And Miles had a cantankerous sensibility that was oddly appealing at first, but I imagined it was one that could easily grow stale.

"So Miles," I began. "I understand you have a problem you'd like me to look into."

"I need a snoop," he declared.

"I prefer the term Private Investigator."

"Eh. Call yourself whatever you want, Burnside. I just need someone to go undercover in my warehouse. I'm losing thousands of dollars in product every week."

"I thought you just installed Cable TV systems."

"We do. We're what's called a home service provider. We hook customers up, install the set-top boxes in the homes. But the boxes are starting to disappear like crazy. I know who's doing it, I just can't prove it."

"Have you set up security cameras?"

Miles gave me an incredulous look. "Do I strike you as an idiot? Of course I did. The thieves wore masks and spray-painted the camera lens. I know who it is. I'm having Union problems and the shop steward has been a constant thorn in my side during bargaining talks. I'm sure he's behind it somehow."

I sat back for a minute and took all of this in. "You can put in a second set of surveillance cameras. Make them covert. They get activated when the first ones are tampered with. Mount them high up."

Miles thought about this. "That's an idea," he said.

"I understand this is a family business."

"Oh yeah," he nodded. "Peter and Isabelle run the day-to-day. But I'm still the one in charge."

"Your kids work in the business?"

"Yup. Well, two of them, anyway. Got a third kid, the youngest, he decided to move to New York. Works as a consultant on Wall Street. Didn't want to work for his old man, he wouldn't even go to SC. Eddie was always the kid who did things differently."

"Was that disappointing?"

"Eh, it was a long time ago. But in some ways I respect Eddie the most."

"Because he made it on his own."

"Yup. Just like me. Nobody handed me nothing. In fact my old man kicked me out of the house when I was 18. Forced me to be an adult. I wanted to do that favor for each of my kids. Sink or swim. But Clara stopped me."

Clara laughed. "I'm all for being self-sufficient. But you need to help your children get a decent start in life. And sink or swim isn't the best method for everyone. It can lead to a lot of problems down the road."

"Oh heck, Clara, I just wanted to teach them the value of a dollar. My old man used to have me mow his lawn. Paid me 5 cents for a couple hours' work."

"Not a great wage," I said. "No matter what era you grew up in."

"Nope. But I used that nickel each week to buy me a chocolate bar. And it always turned out to be a damn good chocolate bar as a result."

"I didn't think that was the parenting model I wanted to follow," said Clara. "But a child should understand the importance of money, and you do have to earn it."

"So all your kids have successful business careers?" I asked.

"Yeah. They do okay," Miles said. "Maybe not as good as me. But I'm a tough act to follow."

Clara put a hand on my shoulder. "Do you have a family, Burnside?"

I shook my head. "Haven't found the time yet."

She nodded slowly, her helmet of white hair bobbing up and down. While there was a ruddy toughness to her demeanor, she maintained the last traces of what was once a beautiful face. "Found the time for a girlfriend?"

I smiled. "Yes. Gail. In fact she's flying back down here later today. Been interviewing for a job and visiting friends. She just finished law school recently. Up north."

"I'll bet it's tough to have a long distance relationship," Clara said.

"We're used to it," I sighed. "She's been at Berkeley for the last three years."

Miles turned to me with a pained look. "She's been going to school with them socialists?"

I shrugged and didn't respond. Since Miles didn't take kindly to my having a girlfriend who had gone to Cal, I decided not to make things worse by telling him Gail had been an undergraduate at our cross-town rivals in Westwood.

We stopped talking for a moment and stood up to watch the opening kickoff. The game began on a sour note for the Trojans. Cal's kickoff returner caught the ball near the goal line, and began moving up the middle of the field before cutting sharply to the near sideline. Outrunning everyone in the coverage, he scampered untouched all the way into the end zone for a 99-yard touchdown. Within seconds, USC was losing 7-0.

"Bad karma, Miles. You should have let those Cal people wear their caps."

"Heck no," he scowled. "It's un-American. Don't worry.

We'll take control of this game soon enough. I have a good feeling about today."

I did too. It had been a few years since I had sat in 50-yard line seats, and it was a treat I wanted to savor. When my old teammate Johnny Cleary was named head coach, he had offered me some sideline passes if I would come in one day and address the team. He wanted to bring back some of the old time Trojan spirit. I told him I would be happy to do it, and with the season winding down, I needed to get back to him soon and keep my promise. As well as working in time for my new client.

"So Miles, I'll stop by your office this week and we can discuss how to approach this."

"Good."

"I just hope we don't get tossed out of the Coliseum today. I'd like to see the end of the game."

"I promise. But I can't vouch for Clara."

"Oh? Has she popped anyone?"

Clara sat back and grinned. "Nope. But I came close last year."

I raised my eyebrows. "You almost got into a brawl?"

Clara gave a devilish smile. "Oh, it wasn't a fight. Last year a couple of young men in the row in front of us decided they wanted to watch the game standing up. I gave one of them a good poke with my umbrella and told them to sit down. They started whining about their rights, too."

Miles chuckled and broke in. "That's when Clara really jammed the umbrella into one of them. Told them if they didn't sit down they wouldn't have any ribs left by halftime."

"I take it they sat down."

"Oh they did. They said they paid hundreds for their seats and I told them we've paid millions to begin the Coliseum renovations. They weren't going to top that."

I doubted many others would either. I looked at Clara. "Glad Miles didn't have to slug anyone."

"I'm glad too," she smiled. "But I think those fellas were more worried about me."

To purchase the full copy of Bubble Screen, please visit www.Amazon.com

Fade Route

www.ingramcontent.com/pod-product-compliance
Lightning Source LLC
Chambersburg PA
CBHW020616260626
47157CB00003B/1036